SEDUCING MY GUARDIAN

A TOUCH OF TABOO NOVEL

KATEE ROBERT

TRINKETS AND TALES LLC

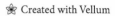 Created with Vellum

ALSO BY KATEE ROBERT

Forever Theirs

Theirs Ever After

His Forbidden Desire

Her Rival's Touch

His Tormented Heart

Her Vengeful Embrace

The Kings Series

The Last King

The Fearless King

The Hidden Sins Series

The Devil's Daughter

The Hunting Grounds

The Surviving Girls

The Make Me Series

Make Me Want

Make Me Crave

Make Me Yours

Make Me Need

The O'Malley Series

The Marriage Contract

The Wedding Pact

An Indecent Proposal

Forbidden Promises

Undercover Attraction

The Bastard's Bargain

The Hot in Hollywood Series

Ties that Bind

Animal Attraction

Come Undone Series

Wrong Bed, Right Guy

Chasing Mrs. Right

Two Wrongs, One Right

CHAPTER 1

$\mathcal{I}$ used to be a good girl. The apple of my parents' eyes, their precious daughter who could do no wrong and only wanted to make them happy. The over-achiever who got good grades, always did extra credit, and never stayed out past curfew.

Why would I cause trouble? I had the perfect life, after all. The perfect house on its quiet private street with it's perfect climbing tree in the front yard and acres to explore and play in. The perfect parents who were strict but loving and never, ever fought. The perfect circle of private school friends since kindergarten. Even the perfect boyfriend, kind and sweet and always respectful.

Everything changed on my sixteenth birthday.

A rainy night. A too-sharp turn. Glaring headlights in the windshield.

Sometimes I feel like I woke up in another world after the car crash that killed my parents. One where up is down and down is up. A life where I have no living parents, no house, no friends. Where I have *nothing*.

Except Devan.

He showed up a few days after the crash. I'm still not sure why my parents chose *him* as my guardian, an old army buddy of my father's, one who was a stranger to me. Maybe they never expected anything to happen to them. People rarely do.

I was so numb during that time, I don't remember much. Just that Devan mostly ignored me in favor of dealing with the endless details of my parents' funerals and wakes and, god, I don't even know. And that he was handsome enough to launch a thousand fantasies. Even grief-stricken and wrapped in a cold that still plagues me to this day, I noticed *that*.

The day after my parents' funerals, Devan bundled me up, shipped me off to boarding school, and has proceeded to ignore me for the past nine years.

Except when I get into trouble.

It was three years after that horrible birthday when I first figured out how to get his attention. A friend had the brilliant idea to hop on a plane to Mallorca to party for a long weekend. To get me out of my head and chase away the ghosts surrounding the day of my birth. I was nineteen, after all, and needed to have some fun. Fun. The entire concept was laughable then, and it's laughable now.

Fun is for people with parents. *Fun* is for people who don't have gaping holes in their chest where love used to reside.

I had nothing better to do, so I endeavored to have *fun*. Too much fun. Too much alcohol. Too much sun. Too many handsome Spanish men with too friendly hands.

At least I was feeling something.

I was doing body shots in a string bikini when Devan appeared like some kind of reaper, hauled away the guy licking his way up my stomach. He took off his button-down shirt, wrestled my belligerent drunk ass into it, and took me back to college.

At that point, I'd convinced myself that he couldn't possibly be that handsome, that it was all a fiction my traumatized sixteen-year-old brain had created in the midst of the worst trauma of my life. Silly me. Of course he was that handsome, of course he was even colder than I remembered.

So I did it again for my twentieth birthday. A frat costume party, because of course. I was dressed in the sluttiest schoolgirl costume I could find, a request from my boyfriend at the time. Devan scared the guy so bad he almost pissed himself, and shuttled me home safely. Again.

It became a tradition. I stopped asking him why he showed up. His sudden presence on a single night of the year became a compass of sorts for me. No matter what else was going wrong in my life, at least Devan cared enough to show up and make sure I don't drink myself to death on the one night of the year when I can't stand being in my own skin.

The rest of the time?

I'm just a spoiled little rich girl. Too much money. Too many friends who aren't really friends at all. Too many boys who want my body, but flit away the second they realize I'm damaged goods.

It's time to grow up and put my wild streak behind me. To finally stop pining after a man who's nothing more than a ghost that manifests a single night of the year. I'll never truly escape the night my parents died. Trauma like that writes itself into your very bones. But that doesn't mean I have to wrap myself in the chains of grief and let it pull me under. Not anymore.

I promised my therapist I'd stop using my birthday as an excuse to cut myself open just so I can be sure I still bleed.

Later. I'll do all the right things later.

Tonight, though? At midnight, my twenty-fifth birthday

begins. The nine-year anniversary of my becoming an orphan. No one can tell me those aren't auspicious numbers. I plan to make it one for the record books. A birthday to put all my others to shame. One to finally get whatever closure I can.

I'm an adult, after all. I have been for a long time.

I don't need Devan playing the part of my savior anymore. I don't *want* it.

What I *do* want is forbidden. Nine different kinds of wrong for the nine years I've been an orphan. The nine years he's been my distant guardian.

I want Devan. Only for a single night. What better way is there to put the past behind me once and for all? Surely I'm not the only one who's felt the tension snapping between us during our rare moments together? Surely I'm not the only one who's harbored breathtakingly hot fantasies about what we'd do if his control ever slipped?

Tonight, I mean to find out.

CHAPTER 2

I smooth a hand down my gown. I've chosen the location of this birthday carefully. This is no rave, no wild club, no particularly intense house party like when I turned twenty. Compared to all my former birthdays, this place is ridiculously respectful.

This hotel bar is already full despite the relatively early hour, populated by people whose bank accounts make my trust fund look like pocket change. If Devan tries to manhandle me out of here, it will do more than raise eyebrows.

If he comes at all.

I twist on my barstool and pick up my glass of scotch. It's expensive and peaty and oh so pretty as I swirl it in my glass. I don't drink scotch often. It's filled with too many memories and even the good ones are a sharp knife; a breathless moment of release, followed by shockingly intense pain. Even now.

This might all be for naught. Devan has the uncanny ability to sense when I'm about to tip over the edge. I feel that way right now, but it's entirely different than my birthdays since my parents died. I ignore the doubt that arises at that thought. It *is* different. This is closure that I desperately need. A period at the end of so much grief.

Before, I was flinging myself headlong into a bonfire just to feel something.

Tonight, I'm leaping out of a plane and praying my parachute isn't about to malfunction.

I take a sip of the scotch, letting it play over my tongue. It tastes like bittersweet memories, and my throat gets a little tight in response.

"You're too pretty to be drinking that, darling."

I bite back a sigh of impatience. The trio of men sitting at the table in the corner have been watching me from the moment I walked in. They're all about ten years older than me, and all sporting wedding rings. This foolish soul clumsily slipped off his before he worked up the courage to approach me.

I don't have many standards, especially when I get to feeling too tight for my skin. But there are lines even I won't cross. Hurting myself with my actions is one thing; hurting someone else is something else altogether. I refuse to do it.

"Are you about to tell me that only old men drink scotch?" I hold this stranger's gaze as I lift the glass to my lips and take a long swallow. "Guess I'm not your type."

He stares, alcohol obviously dulling his senses and making it take time for my words to penetrate. Slowly, understanding dawns. His already red face flushes a red so dark, it's nearly purple. "You've got a mouth on you."

"Most people do."

His eyes snag on my lips, painted a crimson to match the gown that hugs my body like a second skin. "Bet you know what to do with it."

I'm already tired of this conversation, already bored with

this man who thinks a dull pick-up line and a short temper are the least bit attractive. "You'll never know."

I turn back to the bar, but I can't help watching him out of the corner of my eye. If he reacted strongly enough to a simple comment about my obvious lack of interest, I doubt he's going to take a clear rejection now. The bartender is occupied with a pair of pretty women on the other side of the room. There will be no help from him. Not that I need help, but getting into a confrontation will ruin my chances of this night playing out how I've planned. I don't know if and when Devan will show up, and the last thing I need is him riding in to save me when I don't need to be saved.

Not this year.

The man draws himself up, and this time I can't stifle my sigh. Confrontation, it is. If I take care of this quickly, hopefully it won't derail the rest of the night. "Look, you seem like a nice guy—"

"Do you know who I am? You can't talk to me like that." He leans forward, getting in my space.

I stare at the bottles populating the wall across from me. They're all top shelf and expensive, even though the presentation is a bit dull. Kind of like this guy. I shrug. "It's a free country. I didn't ask you to come over here. I can talk to you however I damn well please."

"You little bitch. You think you're hot shit, don't you?" His voice goes high and angry. "Look at me when I'm talking to you, bitch."

The air in the bar shifts. I shiver, the small hairs lifting on the back of my neck. *Oh no.* I thought I could take care of this before Devan arrived. I'd half convinced myself he wouldn't show up at all. Looks like I'm wrong on both counts.

"Are you listening to me?" The man reaches a rough hand to wrap around my arm.

He never makes contact.

I feel *him* at my back half a breath before Devan grabs the stranger's wrist. "The lady said she wasn't interested." His voice is low, but clear. He also sounds fucking furious.

Damn it.

"Who the fuck are—" he curses as Devan tightens his grip, causing the man's hand to splay out. "Fine. Fuck. She's ugly, anyway."

"Leave." The quiet violence in Devan's tone makes me shiver. If I were smarter, I wouldn't find that so attractive. I certainly wouldn't be quietly delighted by him defending me, even though it's going to make accomplishing my goals for tonight that much more difficult.

He came.

Victory makes me lightheaded. So much so that I nearly miss his next words. "Get up. We're leaving."

Leaving. Because he's not here for me, not really. He's here to bundle me up and cart me to safety like he's done for the last six years. I can't let that happen, and him interceding just now is only going to make this look like it's just another birthday.

I have one chance to get things back on track. I can't yell or get dramatic or cause a scene. That will just confirm to Devan that he's right and I'm in trouble. The only option is to not give him anything to work with. The bartender finally returns to the bar itself and I motion him over with a smile. "Another, please."

"Hazel." The warning in Devan's tone makes my thighs clench together. "You're going home."

No. I am most certainly *not* going home. Not alone. "Can't go home," I say breezily. "Home is a few thousand miles away." At least one of them.

"You have an apartment a few blocks from here."

Of course he knows that. He's the executor of the trust fund I inherited with my parents' death. He's been painfully responsible with it; from what my financial advisor tells me, I have even more money now than I did upon my parents' death because of Devan's careful investments. He never meets with *me* about money. All my requests go through the financial advisor. Not that Devan tells me no often. He doesn't tell me anything at all.

That would require speaking to me.

I check the diamond watch on my wrist. Not much longer now.

"Hazel."

"Have a drink with me, Devan." I lift my glass. "For old time's sake."

"Hazel." Something filters into his tone, something besides barely restrained irritation. Devan looks around, seems to clock how many people are watching us. "You're going to be difficult, aren't you?"

I smile, though my chest hurts a bit. "I'm told I'm always difficult."

He turns back to me, that strange look still lingering in his dark eyes. Finally, he sighs. "One drink and then I'm putting you in a cab."

Yeah, I don't think so. I almost laugh, but he won't appreciate it. I've only won the first encounter; it will take a lot of doing to win the war itself. The bartender chooses that moment to appear with the second drink. He sets it on the bar and moves off without a word.

I sip my scotch. "You know, it's very stalkerish that you keep figuring out where I am on my birthday. Seems like a lot of work without much payoff."

Devan glares at his drink as if it insulted his mother. "Don't play innocent, Hazel. It doesn't suit you. All I have to do is look you up on social media. You post your location for the entire world to see."

"Oh. That." I smile against my glass. I always, always post

leading up to my birthday and tag my location. I have ever since that first birthday in Mallorca. "It makes sense for me to post so often. I make a lot of money on social media sponsorships. They like to send me places. Nothing strange about that." It wasn't something I was overly into in my teens, but there's a certain high that only a perfectly curated social media feed can deliver. I've even started designing them for other people and making a good living at it. Not that I need the money, but I like the work.

"You're a menace." He says it so softly, I don't think he means for me to hear it.

He has no idea.

We drink in silence for several long moments. Or, rather, I drink and Devan watches me. Now that the time is upon me, my courage wavers. Just because Devan has been such a huge, if contained, part of my life doesn't mean he feels the same way. I very well could have imagined that spark that seems to sizzle between us whenever he gets too close. Just like I could have misinterpreted what happened on my last birthday...

I close my eyes and steel my nerves. No. I didn't misinterpret. I'm nearly certain of it, but there's really only one way to find out and it involves shooting my shot in a way he can't ignore. "I'm not getting in a cab, Devan."

"Yes, you are."

"No, I'm actually not." I twist on my barstool to face him, only stopping when my knees connect with his. The tiniest of touches, but it shoots through me like a bomb going off. "It's almost my birthday."

"I'm aware." His thigh tenses, but he doesn't otherwise move... Not even to shift away.

"You're early. Normally you don't show up until the day of, and you at least let me have some fun before you show up to act like the birthday Grinch." Though I doubt what happened last year could be called *fun* by any definition of the word. Fun is light and fluffy and maybe a little chaotic. My last birthday was fiery and burrowed beneath my skin in a way I'm afraid I'll never escape. I've certainly fantasized about it often enough.

Best not to think about that if I want to keep my focus.

"Strange way to say thank you."

"Because I'm not saying thank you," I snap back. "I never asked you to come looking for me, and I never asked you to save me."

Devan stares at the wall of bottles behind the bar. "You needed saving."

As much as I want to argue, it's the truth. I was free falling for a long time after my parents' death, and even when I finally found my feet, the one day of year certain to send me into a tailspin is my birthday. Every single fucking year. So maybe he's a tiny bit right about my needing saving. "There *may* have been a few times when you were helpful."

He finally meets my gaze, and my breath catches in my throat. He's so fucking handsome, I can barely stand it. A thick body that might give really good hugs or might just allow him to rip someone's head clean off. Dark hair that's a little too long and showing no signs of graying, despite the fact that he has to be in his early forties at this point. A really well-maintained beard that smelled like cloves last year when I had my face buried in his neck while he carried me.

I can't read Devan's expression clearly. All I know is that it's intense. He speaks in a low voice, saying so much with only a single word. "Amsterdam."

"Amsterdam," I agree on a sigh. Twenty-two. Bar-hopping with a bunch of people I'd just met that night, too many drinks; one of which ended up getting dosed with something. I don't remember Devan showing up. I don't remember much of anything at all after taking shots with a

11

group of guys I'd declared my new best friends. The next thing I knew, I came to, draped over a toilet with Devan's hands in my hair, holding it away from my face as I puked my guts out. That's the only time he's stayed longer than to just deliver me to a plane back home. He took care of me.

He's been taking care of me for a long time, though not in a guardian kind of way.

I force myself to hold his gaze. I spent too many years being a total train wreck, but I'm not that girl anymore. Realistically, I have a lifetime of work ahead of me but I've made a lot of progress since twenty-two. I'm putting in my time in therapy, working through all the baggage I've been dragging behind me for far too long.

Then what is tonight about?

I ignore the little voice that sounds remarkably like my therapist. Tonight is about closure. Shutting the door on one part of my life and opening a different door into the future. And...maybe... Maybe I've still got a wild streak, because I *want* this. I want it more knowing I shouldn't have it. "This isn't Amsterdam. That was a bad birthday."

Devan leans forward the tiniest bit, his dark eyes drilling into mine. "Have there been any good birthdays, Hazel?"

I flinch a little. It's a fair question. My first instinct is to avoid it, but that's not fair to either of us. Instead, I take a slow breath and straighten my spine. "I'm hoping this one will be the first."

Devan holds my gaze and takes a long drink of his scotch. He jolts a little. For just a moment, he looks less like a personified storm cloud and more like an actual human. "This is Caol Ila."

That thick feeling in my throat comes back. It feels good and it hurts all at the same time, and somehow that makes everything better. How can a person appreciate the good things if they've never felt the sting of loss? I'll never know. I never got the opportunity to know. "Mmhmm." My smile trembles a little around the edges. "Dad's favorite."

"Yeah." The faintest smile touches his lips. "Yeah, it was." For the millionth time, I wonder how this man became my guardian. I understand that he and my father served in the army together and that bonds a person, but is it really how someone chooses who should raise their child should the worst come to pass? And my mother, the pacifist? I can't imagine her signing off on this choice, especially considering Devan was never *around*, but obviously she did because here we are.

We finish our drinks in silence, and he sets his glass down with a clink. "Let's go."

"Pass." I start to motion to the bartender, but Devan catches my hand in a firm but impossible to escape grip. Not that I'm trying to escape. But giving in too easily won't do, either. I eye where he holds me. "Devan, what time is it?"

He doesn't release me as he checks his watch. "Twelve-fifteen."

I smile. This time, it feels real. Really, truly real. "That means you're no longer the executor of my trust fund. Happy birthday to me." Now's the time for courage, to put it all out there. For better or worse, I'll have no regrets. I lean forward and lower my voice. "Do you know what I'd like for my birthday?"

"What?" He asks warily.

"You."

CHAPTER 3

*D*evan releases me instantly. I stare at my wrist. He wasn't holding me that harshly, but I swear I can feel the imprint of his skin against mine, a perfect replication of his five fingers and palm. He glowers at my empty glass. "How much have you had to drink?"

I fully expected this question, which is why I showed restraint despite my nerves. "Just the one." Honestly, I could have used more for a boost of courage. "I'm not even buzzed."

"Did that fucker drug you?" He starts to turn toward the trio of men in the corner, but I wrap my hand around his forearm. He's just as thick here as he is on the rest of his body. Devan is just a big guy, and a devious part of my mind can't help wondering if he's as thick *there*, too.

The thrill of touching him makes me lightheaded. A small thing, my hand on his forearm, but it feels like the prelude to so much more. Rather, I desperately *want* it to be a prelude to so much more. "Is it so hard to believe that I can be sober and want you?"

"Yes," he says shortly.

"Devan." Now it's my turn to inject censure into my tone. Who the hell could look at this man and *not* want him? Sure, he's not ripped, and he's got a shitty attitude, but there is more to life than sunshine and muscles. He's got a presence that dominates the room. Even without all that taken into account, he can't pretend not to know that *I* want him. "I may have been blitzed last year, but I remember *everything*."

A faint flush colors his cheeks and his jaw goes tight. The tiniest of reactions, but he might as well have held up a glitter sign saying he's affected by me, too. "I should have stopped you."

I'm so very glad he didn't, for all that the memory brings as much embarrassment as it does desire. "But you didn't." I say it softly. "Surely I didn't imagine how closely you watched me the entire time. You can't pretend *that* was purely for safety reasons."

"I should have stopped you," he repeats.

"I'm glad you didn't." It's the truth. I've never been able to quantify what I feel for Devan. It's messy and confusing and I've hated him at times. But there's no denying the craving I have that goes beyond simple desire.

It's pure lust.

Last year, that lust bubbled over into action; at least on my part. It takes barely any effort at all to be right back in that memory of us in the backseat of that town car. Of the sound he made when my skirt slid up to reveal my panties. It should have stopped there, but I've never been on that great of terms with control. I wanted to see if he'd stop me or... maybe take over for me. So I slid my hand into my panties and brought myself to a messy orgasm while he sat there, his body so still it might as well have been a statue. No, he didn't touch me that night. But, god, he *watched*.

I've masturbated to the memory of that sound he made and the heat in his eyes more times than I care to admit.

"Don't stare at me with that look on your face, Hazel. The answer is no."

"But—"

"*No.*"

Disappointment lashes me. I knew this was a possibility, of course. I've been fucking up this man's life once a year for the last six years. He might feel larger-than-life to me, but he's only human. I suppose I could have read too much into his reaction last year. Damn it. I sigh and lean back. Did I really expect him to say anything different? He's never wanted *me*, even if he's always done his duty. Demanding more of him after he's already dealt with so much is too selfish, even for me.

I couldn't have moved forward without shooting my shot, and it sucks that it wasn't received well, but at least I won't spend the rest of my life wondering if I should have at least *tried*. Disappointment won't kill me tonight; it never has in the past. "Okay."

He narrows his eyes. "Okay," he repeats. "Glad we got that cleared up."

"Same." I turn and signal the bartender before he can stop me. It's my birthday and I'll be damned if I spent my first night free being bundled into a cab and sent home early. "Guess it's time for Plan B."

If anything, his eyes narrow further. "I'm not going to like Plan B."

"Probably not, but as I'm twenty-five and you've washed your hands of me, you don't really get a say." I smile at the bartender as he delivers a second drink to me. "Thanks, darling. Nothing for the grump next to me."

"Hazel." That delicious thread of warning in my name. "Explain."

"Oh, right." I don't take a drink, but I do pick up the glass. "I decided that since it's my twenty-fifth birthday as of right now, it's time to celebrate properly. I can't do that alone. I'm taking someone home tonight. Not *home*-home, but I've booked a hotel room. Safety first and all that."

Devan blinks. He looks a bit like a cat that just got swatted with a newspaper. "If not me, then someone else. Just like that."

"Did that sting your pride?" I give him a slow smile, though my chest aches still from the rejection. "I'd prefer to take you upstairs and rock your world until dawn, but if you're not interested, I'm sure someone in this bar is."

"I never said I wasn't interested." He stops short, but finally curses. "It's not appropriate."

Now it's my turn to blink. "Appropriate." I should let it go. Despite the spoiled rich girl routine, I *do* know how to take "no" for an answer. Devan has most assuredly told me no. Pursuing this further is a recipe for disaster.

Except...he just opened the door he slammed in my face two minutes ago.

I shake my head, trying to focus. "Devan." I promised myself I would let it go, that I would keep things even remotely classy, but how am I supposed to keep myself from responding to *that*? Appropriate? The very concept is laughable. "You watched me masturbate in the back seat of a car last year. Are you really going to argue about what's *appropriate* right now?"

His eyes go molten for the breadth of a moment before he locks it down, but it's too late. I've seen it. Holy shit, I *didn't* imagine his reaction that night. Devan McGuire... wants me. A whole hell of a lot, if that look was anything to go by.

He glances away. "Like I said before; that shouldn't have happened."

I want to argue. I want to argue so badly, I have to press my lips together to keep the words internal. I will not beg. I refuse to. If he's determined not to cross the line with me, that's his choice. "Okay."

"Now that we got that cleared up—"

I shake my head. "No. Try again. Like I just said, if you're not interested, that's okay. You're no longer my guardian. You no longer have to feel some obligation to track me down or worry about what I'm doing. But if you are not my guardian and you don't want to fuck me, that means you have absolutely no say in what I do with the rest of my night."

"Hazel."

I give his shoulder an awkward pat. "Have a nice life. I know I wasn't always graceful about it, but thanks for..." My voice threatens to break and I pause. No. None of that. This is a happy moment, and I might honor the past, but I'm moving on to a bright new future. Tonight is about closure. "Thanks for being a constant, even if it was one night a year."

"Fuck." Devan grabs my drink and downs it. "*Fuck.*"

I don't know what that means, but ultimately it doesn't matter. He's made his call, and now it's my turn to do the same. To let go, once and for all. I force myself to turn, breaking our tiny contact, and survey the room.

There are plenty of interested eyes turned our way. Not all of them are aimed at me, of course. Devan is good looking in a rough and brutal kind of way. It's more than just his physical looks; it's the way he moves, the way he owns every room he walks into. For a long time, I thought I was the only one who reacted to him that way, but the last few birthdays have proved me wrong. When Devan steps through the door, people stop and take notice.

Including everyone in this room.

There's a gorgeous older woman at a table in the corner, nursing a glass of white wine. She's in an elegant dress, draped in diamonds, and has wavy dark hair. She's also staring at Devan with enough heat to make *me* blush.

"Maybe neither of us will leave alone tonight," I murmur. No reason to feel the slightest bit of jealousy. No matter what my fantasies encompass, I have no more claim on this man than he has on me. We're simply two people hurtling through life who were thrown into a collision course neither of us asked for.

"Hazel." His hand closes around my thigh and he uses the hold to spin me back to my former position, my knees against his. He searches my face. "You're trying to provoke a reaction."

"Only a little," I admit. I am not a perfect person, but I try very hard to be honest. Most of the time. "Though, contrary to popular belief, I do know how to take 'no' for an answer. You aren't interested, so this is over. End of story."

His gaze drops to my mouth. "Just like that."

"Yes, just like that. Devan." His name feels sinful on my tongue. "You keep saying you're not interested. I keep trying to respect that. Why are you still arguing with me?"

"You don't know what you're asking for."

An illicit thrill goes through me. "Don't I?" I lean forward, nearly whimpering when I catch a faint hint of the oil he uses in his beard. It *is* cloves. I shiver. "I'm no innocent."

"I'm aware of *that*." His voice drops. "I'd be the worst kind of bastard to put my hands on you."

I can't pretend I had the best of intentions coming here tonight, making a big show of celebrating my birthday at midnight. I knew Devan would come for me, just like he always has in the past. I *knew* there was an attraction between us. In this moment, it feels like we're wavering on the edge of something big. All we need is one good shove to send us past the point of no return. "I'm hoping you'll put more than just your hands on me."

CHAPTER 4

*H*e curses. "You don't know what you're asking for," Devan repeats.

I lift my glass and take a long drink. "If you're not interested, that's fine. No harm, no foul. I'm not going to cry myself to sleep over it." *Liar.* "But don't you dare pretend that you're doing it to protect me. I'm an adult and can make my own decisions."

"Hazel." He exhales slowly and glances away. "Look, I don't know if there's some white knight shit going on in your head, but that's not me. I'm not going to lay you down in a bed of roses and make sweet love to you."

Thank god. I wouldn't know what to do with that sort of thing. I don't need a savior, no matter what he thinks. I snort. "Cute speech."

"I'm serious."

"So am I." I set my glass down. "Devan, we might not know each other well when it comes to all the mundane little trivia you pick up on the first three dates, but we *know* each other." I lean forward until we're kissably close. "If you'd stop to really consider it, you'd recognize that I would eat a white knight alive." I hold his gaze, my heart in my throat. "Just like I know that you are more than capable of handling whatever I throw at you."

"Hazel."

"Let me finish please." I draw in a shuddering breath. "But none of that matters."

Devan hasn't seemed to breathe the entire time I spoke. He leans forward the tiniest bit, closing the distance between us a nearly imperceptible amount. "What matters, Hazel?"

Every time he says my name, it's like he's stroking his fingertips down my spine. I try for a smile but can't quite manage it. "The only thing that matters is that I trust you. And I know I'm safe with you."

He curses, low and furious. "That's not fair."

"I know." I never intended to play fair. Not when it comes to Devan or what I'd like to happen tonight. *Especially* now that I know he wants me; he's just being held back by some strange moral code that I want nothing to do with. I hold his gaze and start to lean back, conveying a silent challenge.

He moves before I get a chance to go far. Devan clasps the back of my neck, holding me in place. It's not a rough grip, but there's a promise of roughness there that makes me shiver. He drags his thumb lightly down the side of my throat, his eyes going hot. "You're sure this is what you want?"

"Yes." No hesitation. Why would I hesitate? It feels like this moment, this night, is six years in the making. It feels inevitable.

"What's your room number?"

The question, so practical, so *real*, throws me off. I blink. "Um, right now?"

Devan searches my face, his thumb continuing that intox-

21

icating stroke up and down my throat. "Let me tell you how this is going to go. If it works for you, then we move forward. If it doesn't, I'll put you in a cab and send you home safely."

I can barely draw in a breath. "Okay."

"No games, Hazel. If this isn't for you, you don't get to threaten to fuck other people or double back. Promise me."

I enjoy needling him quite a bit, but I also want *this* more than I want to be a little brat. Which leaves me with a single option. I nod, achingly aware of how the motion rubs the pads of his fingers against my skin. "Okay. I promise."

His lip curve, and anticipation licks through me. Devan leans closer and lowers his voice. "You're going to slip me your spare key and go up to that room. There, you're going to take off that red dress, close your eyes, and bend over that bed and wait for me."

I lick my lips. The room feels like it's become twenty degrees warmer in the last few seconds. *Is this really happening?* "And then?"

"And then I'm going to do whatever the fuck I want to that tight little body of yours." His hand tightens on my neck the slightest bit. "You tell me yellow if we need to slow down, red if you need me to stop."

The room seems to compress around me. My body goes hot and tight. "A safe word." I'm familiar with them, of course. I've had my fair share of adventurous sex games, but I figured out relatively quickly that kink demands more vulnerability than I'm willing to give and should be reserved for special people or special occasions.

Tonight fits both categories.

"You said you feel safe with me. No matter what happens next, that won't change." He holds my gaze. "This only goes as far as you want it to."

The hysterical urge to laugh nearly overwhelms me. He won't thank me for the reaction, will probably even take it the wrong way. This only goes as far as I want it to? I want it to go all the way. I want every single fantasy rattling around in that handsome head of his. Every depraved thing, every dirty little detail. "I want everything." I lick my lips. "I have some fantasies of my own, too."

His gaze drops to my mouth. "You'll tell them to me tonight."

The command makes me shiver, and his gaze sharpens on me, which makes me shiver harder. I hardly sound like myself when I confirm, "I will. I promise."

"Your room number."

I rattle it off without hesitation. My hands are shaking as I pull my spare hotel key out of my clutch and pass it to him. He gives my neck a light squeeze and releases me. "Go."

I go.

I takes more effort than I could have dreamt to keep my pace slow and even as I walk out of the hotel bar. I can feel Devan's gaze on me the entire time, dark and filled with promise.

This is happening.

It's actually—*finally*—happening.

I manage to keep it together until I step into the elevator and the doors slide shut. Only then do I lean against the wall and exhale harshly. "Holy shit. Holy *shit*." Part of me really, truly believed that Devan would turn me down. He's kept himself at such a careful distance since the night we met…

Pain, dull and familiar, lashes me. My parents have been gone a full third of my life at this point. More, even. It still hurts. Not as much as it used to, not enough to send me into a full tailspin every time I accidentally think of them, but the pain is there all the same.

There seem to be no limits on grief.

At least it's faded enough to allow myself to touch on the happier memories. There was a long time where I couldn't bear to think of them at all. I wonder if Devan thinks about my father ever. It's not like we have ever talked about it before, and he lost someone, too. Obviously a friend is different than a parent, but that doesn't mean his grief isn't just as valid as mine.

The elevator doors slide soundlessly open, and I push myself off the wall, letting my momentum carry me out into the hall. The past doesn't matter right now. In a few days, I can go back to the endless slog through grief and working on my mental and emotional health. Tonight is about letting go. Letting *everything* go.

My dress feels obscenely tight as I stride down the hall to the corner penthouse suite. I smile a little to myself. No normal hotel room will do for me, not on this night, not with this man. I wouldn't be me if I didn't make this entire experience an *event*. I even went so far as to plan for success, stocking the room with things we'd need to play out the fantasies that have plagued me for far too long.

Inside the hotel room, I stop and look around. I dropped my things up here earlier, of course, but I only left a single light on the desk turned on. The entire space is bathed in shadows, making it feel both intimate and almost intimidating.

Take off your dress.

Bend over the bed and wait for me.

The memory of Devan's words slide through me, propelling me forward. I wind through the living area and head for the massive master bedroom. My place in New York is bigger than this, but only barely. The sheer opulence is why I chose this hotel, this bar, this room. It feels very grown up and nothing like the partying I've done on every other adult birthday.

Nothing will ever be the same again.

I consider the bedroom and then move to turn on the two lamps on either side of the bed. Enough light to see, but not enough to combat the feeling of illicit deeds done in the dark. Even better, the night sky turns the floor-to-ceiling windows into a mirror. My heart picks up as I look at myself.

I'm conventionally attractive, though my true gift is being extremely photogenic. It's the gift that's paved the way for me to be financially independent, even without the trust fund in play. Add in my tragic backstory, and sponsors are just lining up to be featured to the millions of followers I have on social media.

None of that matters tonight.

I don't care what all those strangers think of my looks, my body.

I only care what Devan McGuire thinks.

It's more difficult than I'd like to get out of my dress. It's a good thing I'm flexible or I'd be screwed. By the time the fabric slithers to the floor around me, I'm breathing hard and regretting my clothing choices. How much time do I have left? Impossible to say.

After the briefest internal argument with myself, I hang the dress up. It's a custom design by a woman who rarely ships outside of her local city; if it gets ruined, I won't be able to replace it even with the resources at my disposal.

I dressed carefully for tonight. I'm wearing a dark red designer balconette bra with the sheerest lace, designed to put my breasts on display more than conceal them. My garter belt and panties are the same crimson shade, but I went with nude stockings. The dress was long enough that stocking weren't required, but I love the look of a garter belt with nude stockings, so I indulged myself. Silver strappy heels complete the image.

I leave the heels on.

After the briefest hesitation, I leave the panties on as well. They're bikini style, but sheer, designed to tease in the same way the bra is. I'm covered, sure, but I might as well be naked.

The bed is situated against the wall across from the door, so when I bend over it, I will be framed by the soft light of the lamps. There's no point in procrastinating. I know I'm going to follow Devan's orders and wait for him, no matter how long it takes. I have more than my fair share of pride, but it has no place in this moment.

With a slow inhale, I bend at the waist and brace myself on my forearms on the bed. The air conditioning teases my exposed skin, raising goosebumps in its wake. As tempting as it is to close my eyes, I'm a showwoman at heart. I turn and look at my reflection in the window.

The position and heels have my ass in the air, my body a long line of invitation. My breasts are currently trying to escape the lace of the bra, and my hair is a messy waterfall on the dark comforter. I bite my bottom lip and spread my legs a little. I can't see *that* angle from here, but Devan will.

If he ever shows up.

No, I can't afford to think like that, to let doubt creep in. He wouldn't have sent me up here if he didn't intend to follow, to… How did he put it?

I'm going to do whatever the fuck I want to that tight little body of yours.

Will he be rough? Fuck, I hope so. I want to be fucked, put in my place, maybe degraded the tiniest bit. Everyone treats me like I'm this golden princess, untouchable and meant to be put on a pedestal.

Devan won't hesitate. I'm certain of it.

But… Just in case…

I straighten and move to my clutch—to my phone. If he's going to leave me in agony waiting for him, it's only fair to spread a little of that agony around. I consider my options and then lay on the bed on my back. The lighting creates a soft, intimate image of my body on my phone. I angle it carefully, and turn the video on.

A slow pan across my mouth, down my chest to where my nipples are clearly visible through the sheer red lace. I catch the edge of the fabric and tug it down just enough to see the edge of one before I continue the path south over my body, following my hand with the camera. It's a little awkward, but I'm a fucking professional and I give exceedingly good sexy selfies.

I skim over the garters and create a V with my fingers, framing my pussy, my slit clearly visible through the panties, for a long moment before I end the video.

I've had Devan's number for years, but the only text exchange we've ever had was after my twenty-first birthday when I cussed him out for stopping me mid-threesome. The memory makes me smile a little, especially when I skim back over the texts. I was so *furious*, and only partially because of an aborted orgasm from the girl going down on me.

The last text makes me laugh a little.

Me: You owe me a goddamned orgasm, Devan. I mean it.

He never responded, of course. And when I sobered up the next day, I spent several hours debating whether I should apologize or just pretend it never happened.

Now, I really hope there's an orgasm—many orgasms—in my future. I bite my bottom lip and send the video to him. Once it shows as delivered, I silence my phone, drop it onto the chair next to my clutch, and resume my position on the bed.

It's not long before a sound catches my attention. The beep of the keycard in the hotel room door. The soft sound of it opening. The heavier tread that I recognize down to my very soul.

Devan is here.

CHAPTER 5

$\mathcal{I}$ hold perfectly still as I listen to him walk through the hotel suite. He's not moving quickly, but he's also not meandering, either. A few seconds later, he stops in the doorway of the bedroom. I don't twist to look at him, don't do anything but hold my breath.

"Look at you," Devan murmurs. "Apparently you *can* follow simple orders."

My eyes snap open. I'm not sure when I closed them. "Excuse me?"

"You heard me." A step, and then another.

I turn my head and watch him in the reflection. Devan slowly shrugs out of his jacket, his gaze pinned on my ass. He tosses the jacket onto one of the two chairs situated next to the bed. He slides out of his shoes and kicks them aside. I press my lips together against the demand that he strip further, that he expose himself the same way I'm exposing myself right now.

The way I did in that video I sent him.

"Did you like my text?" The question pops out before I can think better of voicing it.

Devan doesn't move closer. "You wanted that little tease of a video to have me sprinting up here and fucking you like an animal." He slowly pulls off his sweater, and then the T-shirt below it.

Devan McGuire is shirtless in my hotel room.

I worry my bottom lip even as I have to concentrate to keep my legs spread instead of pressing them together in response to the sight that greets me in the reflection. He's so *big*. Barrel chest, solid thick stomach, biceps that scream so much strength, it makes me weak in the knees.

He finally closes the distance between us and presses his fingertips to the small bit of skin exposed between the back of my garter belt and the top of my panties. "This might come as a surprise to a little brat like you, but you're not in charge here, Hazel. I am."

My heart flutters strongly enough to be alarming. "What are you saying?"

"I'm saying you've been a hellion for nine long years, and it's time someone put you in your place."

Yes, yes, yes. "I'd like to see you try."

His low chuckle has things clenching low in my body. "Trust me, I'm going to do more than try." He drifts his fingers lightly over the lace of my panties, down the center of my ass and shifting to the side before he reaches where I desperately need him. I make a sound of protest and push back against his touch.

Devan swats me lightly on my ass. "First thing's first. You have anything you're certain you're not down for?"

"I'm down for anything." I say it mostly to annoy him.

He snorts. "Try again, brat. Everyone has limits."

"Not everyone." But ultimately he's right to ask this question and I owe him honest answers. Devan's just ensuring we both have a good time, and brat or not, I'm in total agreement. "I don't want to be blindfolded."

He goes still, which is right around the time I realize he was tracing the edges of my panties. "Okay."

I appreciate that he doesn't ask why, but then I expect he already knows. After the car crash, I sustained a head injury and they'd had a bandage around my eyes when I woke up. I shudder as the remnants of that memory echo through me. Ever since then, I can't stand to have my eyes covered. No sleep mask, no cucumbers over my eyes, nothing.

"What else?"

I huff out a breath. "I like some pain play, but I've mostly kept it to spanking or paddling in the past. I'm not saying no to the more extensive things, though. There aren't any role-playing scenarios off the top of my head that I can think will be triggering."

"Daddy, doctor, teacher?"

I shiver. "Not triggering."

"Mmmm." He lightly squeezes my ass. "If anything comes up, you will tell me."

It's easy enough to agree to that condition. I already did when we first opened negotiations. "Okay."

"Birth control?"

"Yes," I breathe. Like the bar downstairs, the room seems to heat up the longer we're this close. He's barely doing anything to me, but I'm in danger of combusting. "I'm also tested regularly."

"I am, too." He hesitates. "I have condoms, though."

"Optimistic of you."

"I like to be prepared." He makes a low sound. "Though I wasn't prepared for *this* tonight." He traces the back straps of the garter belt. "We should use condoms. It's the smart thing to do."

There is nothing smart about what we're doing tonight. It's reckless in the extreme, for all that I'll never see him again. The man was my *guardian* for years, if an absent one. I try to imagine what it would be like living in his house as a hormonal grief-stricken teenager, but my mind rebels at the very idea. It's better this way.

We're both adults.

Nothing to stop two consenting adults from exchanging as much pleasure as they can handle, even if it's only for the night.

I arch my back a little, pressing my ass more firmly against his hand. "I don't want to be smart."

"Hazel—"

My name on his lips is better than any designer drug. I push on, throwing myself past the point of no return and dragging him with me. "I want you to fuck me bare, Devan. I want you to fill me up like the dirty little slut I am. I *crave* it."

His hands tighten on my ass, hard enough to hurt for the barest moment. Then he hooks the edges of my panties and eases them down a few inches. Just enough to tease us both. "Dirty little slut is right. No good girl talks like that. No good girl *wants* to be fucked bare and filled up."

"Being a good girl is overrated."

"Guess I'll have to teach you some manners," he says softly, so softly I'm not sure if he's talking to me or himself. "Until you learn to behave properly. Not bend over and flash your pussy at the first person to walk through the door." He eases my panties down to the lower curve of my ass.

I can't quite draw in a full breath. This is both a game and intensely serious. If I were smart, I'd bend for him, would promise to be a good girl and obedient. The thought sends a bolt of heat through me, but it's nothing compared to the feeling when I imagine pushing back. Play the brat, which doesn't feel much like playing at all. I lick my lips. "If someone else walked through that door, they'd already have their tongue in my pussy."

He tsks. "You're just proving my point." Devan digs his

32

thumbs into the soft flesh where my ass meets my thighs and spreads me. I don't know how much he can see in the low light, but I *feel* exposed when the cold air touches my center.

Abruptly, he releases me and steps back. Dazed, I watch him in the reflection as he strides to the empty chair and sinks onto it. "Come here, birthday girl."

I slowly straighten. My brain is buzzing so hard, it's a wonder I'm able to move at all. After a brief debate, I pull my panties back into place. He's teasing me, and while I can appreciate a good edging should it come to that, it's not in my nature to make things the least bit easy.

I put a little swing in my step as I cross to him. God, the way this man watches me. He drinks in the sight of me like I'm the best kind of scotch, expensive and meant to savor.

I don't want to be savored.

I want to be fucking *railed*.

Devan holds out a hand, a clear command. I reluctantly set mine in his. I barely have a chance to register his grip tightening when he yanks me forward to sprawl face-down across his lap. I shriek and flail, but he plants one large hand across the small of my back, easily pinning me in place.

"What the fuck?"

"Exactly, Hazel. What the fuck?" He palms my ass again. Apparently, Devan is an ass man. Either that, or he's just touching the part of me most easily accessible. I honestly can't be certain of anything when it comes to him. He grips the back of my panties and pulls them back to the exact spot they were earlier. "I didn't give you permission to cover up again."

"Fuck off." I wiggle, mostly to test him, and his thighs tense beneath me, shifting so that I'm high-centered and even more helpless than before.

"Good girls get rewards. Do you know what bad girls get?"

I shiver, my instinct to fight battling with my desire for whatever comes next. "What?"

"Birthday spankings." He brings his hand down on my bare ass before I can brace for it.

I shriek and flail harder. Rationally, I'm more than aware that he's not spanking me that hard. I had a girlfriend who was really into spanking and she could leave me bruised for days. Devan is nowhere near that level of impact. Yet.

None of that matters, though. "Stop."

"Stop doesn't mean stop. Red means stop." He doesn't spank me again, though. I belatedly realize that he's giving me time to react. "Do you want to use red, Hazel?"

Of course not. The struggle is as much part of this game as anything. Humiliation lashes me. I don't want to admit that I want it. I want to fight it and tell him no and have him overpower me. This is just another layer of the game, though. A game that he's as invested in as I am. The evidence of his desire is there, pressed up against my stomach.

I drag in a rough breath. "No, you absolute asshole. I don't want to use red. Or yellow."

"Mmmm." He waits a beat more. Apparently satisfied, Devan says, "You're twenty-five tonight. That was one. Can you handle twenty-four more?"

Jesus. "Only one way to find out."

"You'll keep count." His hand descends again. "Forget your place and we start over."

This time, I don't shriek. I just grind out, "Two."

And so we go. He alternates the strength and placement of each contact, until my entire ass and upper thighs feel like they're on fire. Until tears run down my face and I'm sobbing out each number. Until my pussy is throbbing with every beat of my heart.

"Twenty-five!"

Devan doesn't hesitate. He plunges a single finger into

me. "What a little slut," he murmurs. "Punishments are meant to be endured, not enjoyed."

"Am I being punished for turning twenty-five?" I rasp.

"Yes." He wedges another blunt finger into me. He's just as big here as he is everywhere else and the fit is tight. "You turning twenty-five means I have no claim to you anymore."

I can't move, can't spread my legs because of my panties keeping them trapped together, can't see through the fall of my hair, can't do more than take what he's giving me. "You never did anything with the claim you had on me before now."

Devan twists his wrist and then he's stroking the tips of his fingers against my G-spot. I whimper, the pain radiating from my ass only making me hotter, wetter. "What should I have done, Hazel?" His voice is low, serious. "Should I have ripped off that bikini when you were nineteen and licked your pussy until you came all over my face? Should I have fucked you in the backseat last year? Fucked you *every* year?"

"Yes," I moan. "That's what I wanted. All I wanted." No matter what else is true, this chemistry between us isn't a new thing. "Isn't it what you wanted, too?"

He doesn't answer me with words. He just keeps stroking me on the inside, sending pleasure coiling through me, tighter and tighter. "What I want is for you to come for me. Right now."

It's like his words unlock something inside me. I whimper and then I'm orgasming, my pussy clenching around his fingers. "Oh *fuck*."

"That's it. That's my girl." He keeps stroking, keeps my orgasm coming in wave after wave, until I'm damn near sobbing. Only then does Devan ease his fingers out of me, pull my panties up, and maneuver me up until I'm curled in his lap.

A strange lethargy threatens to drag me down. I lean my

head against his shoulder and let the rhythm of his breathing soothe me. A ragged inhale. A barely restrained exhaled. We're both panting as if we just ran a long distance. At least he's just as affected as I am.

Part of me can't believe this is happening.

Part of me can't believe it took this long.

The night isn't over yet.

CHAPTER 6

*B*eing this close to Devan is strange. We've touched before—hard not to when he's hauling my drunk ass out of bars and parties—but, with few exceptions, he's always been very careful to never linger. Never to let that contact last more than strictly necessary.

Slowly, oh so slowly, my body stops shaking. Only then does he loosen his arms around me and sit back. "Good?"

It's more effort than it should be to dredge up and reply anything other than *more please*. I snort. "As if a little spanking would be enough to put me out. That's barely foreplay."

I feel more than hear his low chuckle. "That *was* foreplay, birthday girl." Devan clears his throat. "Now, will your legs hold, or do I need to carry you?"

That gets me moving. I am made of sterner stuff than to be taken out by a little finger banging and spanking. "I'm fine." I push off his lap, and my knees almost make a liar out of me. My legs shake, but I manage to keep my feet. I very carefully don't look at him, because if he's laughing at me, I might do something ill-advised.

But Devan hasn't moved from his spot on the chair. He watches me out of dark, dark eyes, all amusement gone from his face. "Look at you, Hazel. It's like you were put here on this earth solely to tempt me." His gaze coasts over me, lingering on my face and body with a weight that feels physical.

"I plan on doing a whole lot more than *tempting* you." I want to touch him, to run my hands over his big body and unbutton his pants to release his cock. It's pressing so hard against the front of his jeans, it looks downright painful. I lick my lips. I know just the thing to make it feel better.

I reach for him, but he catches my wrist a few inches from my fingers making contact with his chest. Devan shakes his head slowly. "You haven't earned that yet."

Earned it?

I might laugh if there was enough oxygen in the room. "I want to suck your cock. Surely you're not going to argue about that."

He raises his brows. "You seem to be under the mistaken impression that you're in charge of this encounter. You're not."

"Why deny us what we both want?"

He drags his thumb lightly over my wrist. "Do you send a lot of videos like the one you sent me?"

"You've seen my social media." I shrug. "There's a trick to doing it well, and I'm good at pictures, so why not?"

"Hazel." He tightens his grip even so slightly. "There's a marked difference between what you post publicly and what you sent me. Even when you're mostly naked, it's artsy and shit."

"I'm *mostly* naked right now." I pull against his grip, testing him. My body goes tight and needy when I'm not able to pull free. "And what the fuck are you talking about? That video was high art."

He studies me. "Show me."

"Show you what?"

"You know what."

Yeah, I guess I do. I move to where I dropped my phone earlier and scoop it up. He tugs me down onto his lap the second I get within arm's reach, my back to his chest. I go a little dizzy from touching so much of Devan's bare skin at once. He shifts my hair out of the way and plucks my phone from my hand. I watch, stomach doing somersaults, as he pulls up the camera app.

"Show me," he repeats.

I push the button to flip it to selfie mode and meet his gaze in the screen. Sometimes I get a little turned on when I'm doing photoshoots. Sometimes I do photoshoots just to get myself turned on. Maybe that makes me self-absorbed. I don't know. I don't really care.

I've never felt like *this* before.

"Okay," I whisper. I click the record button.

He maintains a hold on the phone, but I touch the top of it, tilting it until just our mouths are visible and then lower. Devan shifts behind me, and then his lips are against my neck, surprisingly soft against the relative roughness of his beard. I reach with a trembling hand to wrap around his wrist. He allows me to guide him, to bring his hand to my chest, to trail it slowly down my body in the same way I did in the earlier video.

It feels so different now.

Devan's hand is calloused where mine is soft. Not to mention he's so fucking *big*. It makes me shake as he slowly hooks the edge of my bra and tugs it down a little, teasing us both with the sight of my bared nipple.

Then he goes off script.

He presses the phone into my hand. "Hold this."

KATEE ROBERT

"But—" My protest dies as he palms both my breasts. "Okay." This is better. This is so much better.

I can't take my gaze from the screen as Devan touches me. My breasts are plenty large for my frame, but his hands dwarf them. He shifts down a little to play his thumbs over my nipples, drawing them to peaks. "Is all your lingerie like this, or did you put this on special for me?"

"All my lingerie is like this." I shift a little, rolling my hips to rub my ass against his cock. It doesn't matter that I just had an orgasm for the record books, that my skin is still smarting from the spankings. I need more.

So I play dirty.

"I like how I feel in expensive lingerie." I smile a little. "I've never had any complaints from partners."

He sets his teeth against the sensitive spot where my neck meets my shoulders. "Have you worn this for other people, birthday girl? Teased them with your breasts and pussy while playing the innocent?"

I should say yes. I like this thread of jealousy, whether or not it's part of the game. I like the thought of him claiming me in this set and fucking away any fictional memories of other people. I just…can't lie. Not in this. "No." Devan goes still behind me, but I press on. "I picked this out just for you. I wore it just for you."

"Fuck," he breathes. He coasts one hand down the center of my body and cups my pussy through my panties. I follow the move with the phone. It looks just as good as it feels, just as possessive. Devan seems to agree. "Just for me, huh?"

"Yeah."

His hand pulses against my pussy. Not enough contact to get me more than hot and bothered, but it's so sexy, I don't care. "Sure seems like I own this pussy, at least for tonight."

I spread my legs wider. I can't help it. "You do. It's yours. I'm yours." *Just for tonight.* It can only be for tonight. Wanting

40

more than that is absurd and delusional. Devan and I might have shared a very traumatic experience, and he might have been something of an anchor for me during key moments of the aftermath, but we don't have a future. We can't.

He shifts his hand over to grip my thigh. "Show me. Show me what's mine."

I don't hesitate. I reach down with my free hand and tug my soaked panties to the side. I'm so wet from the spanking and earlier orgasm that my pussy shines in the camera. I shiver. "Do like what you see?"

He kisses my neck again, but I can feel him watching the screen. He tugs my leg up and out and then slips his hand beneath me to push two fingers into my pussy from behind.

It felt so good when he did it earlier. It looks a thousand times better to watch his blunt fingers disappear into me. I drag in a breath, but it doesn't matter. I can't breathe, can't think, can't do anything but watch as he slowly retreats, his fingers wet with my desire.

"Yeah, birthday girl." He lifts his fingers slowly, waiting until I follow the movement with the camera, until he presses them to my bottom lip. "I like what I see." He pushes them into my mouth, fucking me slowly here just like he did below. I suck on his fingers, watching the camera, entranced, until he grips my jaw without removing his fingers. The new tension almost makes me gag, and I whimper.

His voice takes on a harsher edge. "You going to give me that pussy you've been teasing me with for so long? I have six years' worth of frustration to take out on this hot little body. You think you can take it?" He eases his fingers out of my mouth so I can answer.

"Do your worst," I rasp.

"Oh, I plan on it." He clasps my throat lightly, bending me back over him. "I should fuck you just like this. Record you taking my cock so I can play it back over and over again." He makes a sound suspiciously like a growl. "Maybe I'll even send it to you every year going forward. Happy birthday, Hazel. Remember the night I played with your pussy until you came so many times, you lost count?"

"Do it."

"There you are, little slut." He says it almost fondly. He uses his free hand to press the button to stop the recording and takes the phone from me, lightly tossing it onto the other chair. "You'd like that, wouldn't you? Years from now, when you're married and settled down and playing the respectable wife, your phone will chime on your birthday and you'll have to go somewhere private to play with your pussy and pretend it's *my* fingers getting you off."

I can picture it all too clearly. Even as part of me cries that I'll never have a *normal* life, that that's the most unbelievable thing about this conversation, I willingly walk down this fantasy road with him. "Why stop there?" I roll my hips again, relishing the sting of his jeans against my ass, the promise of his hard cock *right there*. "Why be satisfied with a video? Maybe my pussy will always be yours on my birthday."

His hand trembles against my throat, but he doesn't otherwise move. "Don't make promises you can't keep."

Except that's exactly what I want to do. My nerves feel over-sensitized and I'm breathing hard. I take the hand not around my throat and guide him to press it back between my thighs. "You've earned it, don't you think? So many years of restraint." He allows me to mold his hand, to push two fingers into me. "One night isn't enough to make up for all that. One night a year is still hardly enough."

"You want to meet me in a hotel bar, slip me your key, and come up here to do all the filthy things your partner wouldn't dream of? You don't have to be respectable with me, Hazel. I know what you really want. What you really *are*."

His lips brush my ear. "While your partner is at home, sleeping in the bed you two share, you'll be here, riding my cock and my mouth and my fingers. Over and over, until you feel like yourself again. Until you can go back to pretending for another long year."

The fantasy hurts and it turns me on, and I don't know if I want to tell him he's an asshole or beg him to make it reality.

"No time like the present to start." Devan shifts his grip on me and then he's pushing to his feet, easily carrying me to the bed. He sets me down on it with more gentleness than I want, and immediately makes it better by winding my hair around his fist and using the hold to tilt my head back. His gaze snags on my mouth. "Hardly know where to start," he murmurs, and I get the impression that he's talking to himself.

"Getting naked sounds like a great plan from where I'm sitting."

"No." A sharp shake of his head. "Don't rush me."

"Devan—"

He tugs on my hair, just hard enough to hurt. "If you won't keep that mouth respectful, I guess I'll just have to teach it a lesson."

Eagerness has me clenching my thighs together. "Oh no," I say drily. "Not that."

CHAPTER 7

*D*evan tugs on my hair again. "I should ask you if you're dating someone, but I'll be honest—I really don't give a fuck. You're mine tonight. Say it, Hazel."

I'm not dating anyone. I'm *never* dating anyone, not in recent years. The people I meet these days who want to seduce or create some kind of relationship aren't interested in seeing beneath the perfectly polished surface. They don't want the ugly bits, the jagged pieces snapped off from the puzzle of the girl I no longer add up to. Devan doesn't want me in any permanent way, and he's already seen me at my worst. The freedom of that knowledge makes me a little giddy. "I'm yours tonight."

"I know." He considers me. "Well, birthday girl. Let's put that disobedient mouth to good use."

I reach for the front of his jeans with shaking hands. I don't think I've *stopped* shaking since he showed up tonight. Desire is a heady thing, and my desire for Devan seems bottomless. Even more so now that I'm dragging down his zipper and working his jeans over his hips. I start to push them down further, but he shakes his head. "That's good enough."

His insistence that we remain as clothed as possible is making me restless. I can't tell if it's a good thing or a bad thing. When's the last time I was denied something I wanted? I can't remember. Oh, there are things that will never be mine again, but these days, if I want it, it's there for the taking.

Except this man.

I just want us both to strip down and to have as much of my skin pressed up against as much of his skin as possible. I wouldn't have thought I was touch-starved, but that's what this feels like. A growing frenzy that Devan keeps intentionally ignoring.

Then nothing else matters because I free his cock and it's *right there*. Just as thick and perfect as the man himself. Big enough that a little tremor of foreboding goes through me. Maybe this extended foreplay isn't a bad thing, because I've never been with anyone this size before. Not even the CEO with the array of rainbow-colored strap-ons. Her largest size was smaller Devan.

I carefully wrap as much of my fist around him as possible. "I don't know if I can take this."

"You can." He doesn't move, just waits for me to decide for myself.

As if I'm going to turn away from him now, giant cock or not. The thought almost makes me laugh. I take a deep breath, do my best to quell my nerves and dip down to take him into my mouth. It's a slow slide, and I immediately make my peace with the fact I won't be able to take him all, or even take this much for long. That's okay. I am more than capable of working with what I have.

"Look at me, Hazel."

I open my eyes and look up his body to his face. He's

staring down at me as if... I honestly don't know. I'm not sure how to define the expression on his face. Intense, yes, but there are layers I'm not capable of peeling back.

It's always been that way with me and Devan. He's the wall I crash against over and over, so strong it seems like nothing I do touches him until, just for a moment, he'll crack a little and the sunlight will stream in.

It feels like that right now. Like I'm being bathed in sunlight.

Then he shuts it down, once more the disapproving asshole. "You should see how you look right now, those pretty red lips wrapped around my cock." He shakes his head slowly. "You're the most fucked up combination of sinful and innocent. It's enough to mess with a person's head."

I ease off his cock enough to say. "Which way do you want me to play?" God knows I can do both; I've angled one or another in the past, though being innocent never felt particularly comfortable. It's not who I am.

"You don't get it." He wraps his free hand around his cock and drags it along my bottom lip. "Be you, Hazel. That's what I want. That's all I want."

He might as well have stripped me down to my skin; further even, down to the flesh, blood, and bones beneath. Burrowing deep to the locked space around my heart. "No one wants that."

Devan lowers his brows. "You don't mean that."

"Please." My throat feels appallingly tight all of a sudden. "We both know it's the truth. I'm not as bad as I used to be, but I'm messy. No one wants that kind of clusterfuck in their lives. Not for long, anyway."

He releases me and sinks down. He's tall enough that we're almost the same height like this, me on the bed, him on his knees. Devan taps my forehead. "Stop that."

"Oh, sure. I'll get right on that. Just, poof, damage gone." I snap my fingers.

His expression goes forbidding and then he clasps my throat, pushing me down onto the bed. I don't fight it. Why would I? I've only played with kink, with dominance and submission, here and there in the past, but I have enough experience to know that I crave the letting go as much as I fear it. The last Domme I played with—the one with all the strap-ons—made me come half a dozen times and somehow that resulted in me sobbing my heart out. She handled it gracefully and took care of me in the aftermath, but that was one experience that deterred me from going deeper into the kink community.

I have no desire to be seen that thoroughly.

With Devan, it's different. He's experienced all my rough edges already. How could he miss them when he's been present for the worst nights of my life?

"That's always been your problem, birthday girl." He drags his hand down the center of my body, stopping just below the waistband of my garter belt. "You think too damn hard. Knock it off."

"Wow." At least I manage to sound sarcastic instead of weepy. "Look at that; you've solved my over-thinking just like you solved my damage. You should charge for your services, Devan. You'd make a killing off poor little rich girls with their sad little broken hearts."

He doesn't answer with words. He simply shoves my legs wide and delivers a stinging slap to my pussy. I shriek and arch up. "What the *fuck* are you doing?"

"Am I interrupting the pity party?" He raises his brows. "Sorry."

"I hate you," I grit out. The slap surprised me more than it hurt, but that doesn't mean I'm about to admit as much. "You're such a dick."

"Keep talking like that and I'll have to punish you again instead of licking this pretty pussy the way we both want. Wouldn't that be a crying shame?"

I open my mouth to snap back, but manage to close it without responding. Is pushing back really worth denying myself the pleasure of Devan's tongue? Of course not.

He massages my thighs lightly, still holding them wide. "You said you have your own fantasies about how tonight plays out. Tell me."

"You want me to tell you...while you're going down on me?"

"Smart girl. Yes, that's exactly what I want."

If he's half as good with his tongue as he is with his fingers, I'm going to have one hell of a time concentrating. "What if now's not a good time? Maybe I want to tell you later."

"You stop, I stop."

I lick my lips. "Okay." I can do this. Surely I can do this.

But as Devan leans down and nuzzles my pussy through my panties, I'm suddenly not so sure. I watch him for a long moment, committing this scene to memory. I know for a fact I'll be rewinding this night over and over again in the future.

He drags his tongue over the sheer lace and pauses. "Hazel." The warning in his tone is enough to loosen my words.

I drop back onto the mattress and whimper as he swipes his tongue over me again. His beard rubs against the bare skin at the top of my thighs above my stockings, and the roughness combined with the slickness of his mouth is enough to have my vibrating. "I want to recreate my birthdays."

Devan pauses. "Explain."

"Don't stop."

His only response is to dip his tongue beneath the side of

my panties. The man is a fucking tease, and I fully intend to return the favor the first chance I get. I moan a little, but I'm not about to do anything to make him stop. "This thing—" I drag in a breath as he spreads me and sucks on my clit through my panties. "This chemistry has been here for years. I want…" Best to just get it out. After what we've already said to each other already, surely nothing is truly forbidden? "I want to recreate my birthdays and do now what I wanted to do then," I say in a rush.

He lifts his head and looks at me. "What did you want to do then, Hazel?"

My skin feels like it's on fire, but I haven't come this far to back out now. "I don't care if you were technically still my guardian, at least of the trust fund. I wanted you to take over for me in the backseat last year. I wanted you to do exactly what you described earlier—rip off my bikini at nineteen and make me come all over your mouth." I can't read the look on his face, so I press on. "I wanted you to follow through on the heat in your eyes when you saw me in that schoolgirl costume at twenty. The threesome at twenty-one. At twenty-two—"

"No."

I blink. "Excuse me."

"Not twenty-two. You didn't need a good fucking that birthday. You just needed to be taken care of, which is exactly what I did."

I want to argue for the sake of arguing, but he's right. There is absolutely nothing sexy about that birthday. "Okay, fine, not twenty-two."

Devan gives me a long look. "Keep going."

"Tell me you didn't want to fuck that body paint right off me at twenty-three."

His gaze goes heated. "I would have to be a monster to touch you while I still had control of your trust fund." He hooks his fingers around my panties and draws them slowly down my legs. "You might have been an adult, but I was technically still your guardian."

"Are you saying you didn't want to fuck me?" As soon as he maneuvers my panties past my heels, I let my legs fall wide. "You didn't think about how good my pussy would feel around your cock? Not even once?" There's something about a garter belt, thigh-highs, and no panties that make me so fucking hot.

From the way Devan looks at me, he feels the same way. His gaze drops to where my remaining lingerie frames my pussy. "Hazel." Again, the warning in his tone.

I mimic it right back at him. "Devan."

"You're playing a dangerous game."

"I have been from the start." I prop myself up on my elbows. "It's only one night. One night of pretending we crossed the line half a dozen times. One night of playing that you're still the guardian who can't stop thinking about what his ward's pussy tastes like. One night of me wanting the single man I'm not supposed to. Tell me that doesn't appeal to you, and we'll drop it."

He coasts his hands up my legs, stopping at the tops of my stockings. "You know that appeals to me."

One last push to get us over the edge. "I have the stuff packed. I can change right now."

He goes still. "You planned for this that thoroughly."

"Hope springs eternal." I *knew* I hadn't misread the chemistry between us, and I wanted to be prepared in case tonight went the best-case-scenario route. I'll never get another chance to play out these fantasies properly again. It has to be tonight. "Please, Devan. Play with me."

A long hesitation. Finally, he sighs. "In a moment."

"But—" My protest dies as he descends on my pussy. I quickly discover that he was merely teasing me before.

There's no teasing now. Devan spreads me wide and kisses me with a devastating thoroughness that has my toes curling. I don't mean to reach down, but then my hands are in his hair and I'm rolling my hips, fucking his mouth even as he fucks me with his tongue.

I want it to last. Dear god, I want it to last.

I've been idling on the edge too long, though. My body takes over and then I'm coming, crying out his name as I orgasm all over his face. He curses against my skin and gentles his kiss almost reluctantly. Devan shoves away from me. "Get changed, birthday girl. If we're going to do this, we're going to do this right."

CHAPTER 8

*A*s I change in the bathroom, I have time to regret insisting on this right now. I should have let him keep charge of things, at least until we had sex. Now my nerves take hold again, and I half expect to step out and find Devan gone, my forbidden fantasies too taboo, even for him.

I check myself out in the mirror. The bikini is identical to the one I wore that birthday, tiny and as red as the dress I had on earlier. The back is cut narrow—not quite a thong, but leaving most of my ass exposed. The triangles of the top are laughably small, barely large enough to keep my breasts contained and cover my nipples.

I drag my hands through my hair a few times, messing up my careful curls and doing a damned good approximation of the beach waves I had going on at nineteen in Mallorca. A tiny bottle of tequila, a sliced lime, and a small container of salt complete the memory. Or they will. I hope.

I take a slow breath, straighten my spine, and leave the relative safety of the bathroom. Devan isn't in the bedroom, but I don't expect him to be. To do this properly, we need the dining room table.

It's only as I'm walking through the hotel room that I realize I have no idea what the fuck I'm doing. This might be my fantasy, but in no part of that fantasy am I in charge of anything. I forgot to tell Devan that, forgot to outline exactly what I want to happen. Then again, I don't *know* what I want to happen. The timeline between body-shot and coming on his cock is blurry.

But as I walk into the main area of the suite, I realize I don't have to worry about anything. Devan's turned off the overhead lights, leaving the lamps on to create a dangerously intimate setting, and there's a faint strain of music from somewhere. It sounds vaguely familiar, and I stop short as realization sets in. "You memorized what was playing that night?"

"Something like that."

I jump a little. I hadn't seen him leaning against the kitchenette counter. He's put his T-shirt back on again, and disappointment courses through me. I hold up the tequila bottle. "I come bearing gifts."

"Mmmm." He motions and I walk over and hand them to him. Devan considers the objects, expression contemplative. "Do you know what I thought when I walked into that place and saw you laid out on the bar, practically naked?"

"No," I breathe. "Tell me."

"I thought..." He lifts his gaze to mine. "I'm dying to know what she tastes like."

I back slowly to the table and lean against it. "Come find out." I test the strength of the table, but of course it holds. Then I sit on it and stretch out. It's a little too short, so my hair and legs drape off on either side, but the sound Devan makes has me fighting for breath.

This is happening.

He starts toward me slowly. I don't know how he manages it, but it's like he flips a switch and sexy menace rolls off him in waves. Just like it did that night. "What's going on here?" I start to sit up, but he plants a hand in the center of my chest and easily pins me in place. "I asked you a question, birthday girl."

"Just celebrating," I breathe.

"Celebrating." He repeats it slowly, as if he's not familiar with the word. "This is how you celebrate? Letting these boys have their mouths all over you."

I bite my bottom lip. "We're doing body shots. You should try it sometime. It might loosen you up."

He widens his hand the slightest bit, his fingers brushing against the curves of my breasts. It's the smallest of movements, and I could almost convince myself it's an accident. Or I could if this was anyone else. "You offering?"

"You see anyone else ready to go?" When he doesn't move, I force out a laugh. Acting every inch the part of the wild nineteen-year-old I used to be. "Thought not, old man. Let me up or get out of the way for the next guy."

His hand tenses on my chest. "Don't move."

I hold perfectly still as he moves back to the counter and then returns with the items I brought in. Devan considers me for a moment. "Salt. Shot. Lime."

"Well, yes, but—"

He presses the slice of lime to my lips, silencing me. Oh, god, why is that so satisfying? I give him wide eyes as I'm actually confused about what's happening. About his intentions. He methodically pours the tiny bottle of tequila into a clear glass. It's not a shot glass, but it will do.

Then he traces his fingers down the string of my swimsuit to the top of the tiny triangle. "Have to do this properly," he murmurs. Before I can dredge up some kind of response, he tugs my top to the side, baring one breast.

I squeak a little, and Devan bends down to suck my

nipple into his mouth. He takes his time, his tongue playing along my skin and over my nipple until it's a beaded peak. Until I'm making little whimpering noises despite my determination to stay silent. Only then does he move back and shake some salt onto the damp area. I'm already breathing so hard, my breasts shake with each exhale, but Devan ignores it. He dips down again and this time, he moves faster. He sucks on my nipple hard enough to make me moan and then his mouth is gone.

Dazed, I watch him down the shot and then he hooks the back of my neck and tows me up to a sitting position. My head spins, and then it spins worse because Devan McGuire is taking a lime out of my mouth. It's not a kiss. It's nowhere near a kiss. That doesn't stop me from digging my hands into the front of his shirt and trying to pull him back to me.

He, of course, doesn't budge. He just looks at me like he's disappointed in me. "So fucking easy to seduce."

The words sting, but somehow the sting makes me even wetter. "No, I'm not." I don't know why I'm protesting. I *want* to be seduced by this man. No, that's not right. I want to be *destroyed* by this man.

"All it takes is some young cocky thing sucking on your nipple and you're panting for it." He slowly plants his hands on either side of my hips, moving forward until I'm forced to spread my legs to allow him. "I bet you'd fuck him right here on the bar, wouldn't you?"

"Not him."

He tugs on the strings of my bikini bottoms. Not enough to undo them. Just enough to tempt me. "Don't act like I'm something special. You didn't expect me to show up here tonight. You're going to let one of those *boys* have his mouth all over you." He leans even closer. "I bet you'd let him take you to that corner booth and fuck him right here."

"No, I wouldn't." I push at his chest, the protest only half feigned. "Give me a little fucking credit. I'm a virgin."

Devan freezes and his eyes go wide. "What did you just say? You're a virgin? How?"

Oh for fuck's sake. He thinks I mean *now?* I brace myself on one hand and lean back, trailing the other hand down my body to brush between my thighs. "Yes, Devan. This nineteen-year-old pussy has never been touched. So no, I won't be fucking just anyone here tonight, so you can mosey on along and let me have my fun."

It takes him a minute to respond. When he does, the shock is gone from his voice. "No, birthday girl. I'm not leaving this virgin pussy here alone. Come on." He moves before I have a chance to respond. Just like that night, he tosses me over his shoulder. Unlike that night, his hand is *very* high up my thigh right now, nearly brushing the lower curve of my ass.

When he drops me down on the couch and sinks down next to me, I shoot up, only for him to hook my waist and pull me back down onto one broad thigh. "We're going to have a conversation, Hazel."

"Great. Fun. Perfect." I struggle a little just to feel the strength of his arm banded across my waist. It makes my swimsuit slide dangerously close to exposing me, so I keep doing it, a slow fight that Devan indulges. Within seconds, my top is askew and my bottoms are loosened on one side, though I'd swear his hand never went anywhere near the ties.

He grips my throat, stilling me. "Look at you. You say you're a virgin, but you're flashing your tits and pussy at anyone who cares to look." His big hand descends to cup me between my thighs. It's a possessive touch and I'm thrilled by it. I'm thrilled even more by his words. "At least cover yourself up before someone takes it as an invitation."

"Someone like you?"

He curses against my temple. "No, Hazel. Not like me. I'm just here to protect you." His fingers flex against my pussy in what seems to be an almost involuntary movement. "It'd be a lot easier to do if you were a good girl."

"What do you mean?" My voice has gone breathy and I've stopped fighting. I carefully grip his big bicep and shift, rubbing my pussy against his fingers. "I'm a virgin. How much more of a good girl can you get?"

"You expect me to believe that when you're rubbing yourself all over me right now?"

"It's not my fault." I don't stop, though. I just swirl my hips a little, trying to get him to make contact with my clit. "It feels too good to stop."

"I damn well should stop." He sounds absolutely tormented. It's so sexy, I almost come on the spot. Devan's fingers flex again. "You should tell me to get my hands off you right this fucking second."

I look across from us, belatedly realizing that he's positioned us in front of the large mirror. "Look at us," I breathe. "Look at how good your hands look on my body."

"I'm your guardian, birthday girl. This is so fucking wrong."

I skate my hands down his arm to his hand. I spread my legs a little wider and tilt my hips and, god, the tips of his fingers slide into me. "It feels better because it's wrong." I press against the back of his hand and he slides his fingers a little deeper. Not deep enough, but doing this in half-measures feels particularly dirty.

"Devan?"

"Yeah," he grits out.

I roll my hips, fucking his hand as much as he'll allow. "I want to have sex so badly. Are you really going to trust that experience with some idiot boy?" I grab his other hand and bring it to one bared breast. "Wouldn't it be better to have

KATEE ROBERT

an older, more experienced man make sure it's good for me?"

"*Hazel.*"

"No one has to know," I whisper. I watch him watch me in the mirror. "No one has to know you're my first. It will be our little secret."

CHAPTER 9

I don't really put must stock in virginity. I gave up religion when I lost my parents, but even if I hadn't, I don't think any gods out there really care about where or not I've had sex. The only ones who seem to care about *purity* are the people intent on controlling young women's bodies. I don't fuck with that nonsense.

I had sex for the first time right before I turned twenty. He was a nice guy who treated me with great care. I think he was more nervous than I was. We dated a few months and then went our separate ways with no hard feelings. So yeah, I don't believe for a second that the first person you sleep with magically links you to them for the rest of your life.

But sitting here, playing out this fantasy with Devan, it feels particularly sexy to lean into those stereotypes, to put far more importance on my imaginary virginity than I ever did on the real thing.

Devan kisses my neck almost furiously. "I should take you to a bed. Should lay you down and touch you gently and treat you the way virgins should be treated."

My breath catches in my throat. "But you're not going

to?" I sound far too hopeful, but I can't help it. *Yes,* a little voice inside me chimes. *Yes, make it dirtier. Treat me like your special little slut.* The truth is that at nineteen, I would have laughed in his face if he tried to take care with me. I was still too raw and drunk on my newfound freedom, desperate for anything, anyone who would make me feel something and help me lose myself for a few hours.

"I should." He shoves two fingers into me. "I'm supposed to take care of you." He fucks me slowly with his fingers, and I've never been so grateful for a mirror before. I'm a visual person. I always have been. Seeing him touch me like this only adds to the pleasure of feeling it happen.

I will never be a woman who wants to fuck with the lights off.

"So take care of me."

Devan keeps finger fucking methodically, working a little deeper each time. Then he adds a third finger. "Can't believe no one's had this pussy before," he growls. "You feel so fucking good, so wet and tight."

"You feel good, too." I'm gasping, writhing around his touch, but he holds me too firmly to do anything but go at his pace. "I need more."

"Need to go slow. Get you ready."

I give a frustrated sound and reach behind me. Devan loosens his hold enough to allow me to undo his pants. All a game. Protest, protest, protest. But we both know the truth; we're both dying to get him inside me properly. I free his cock and freeze. "You're too big." My trepidation isn't entirely feigned. I'd forgotten for a moment. It's going to take *work* to make him fit.

Devan shifts and pulls a small bottle out of his pocket. I frown at it in the dim light. "What is that?"

"Lube. It'll help." He guides me up a bit so he can rearrange his cock to a better angle.

I stare as he spreads lube over himself in economical movements. "You brought lube with you."

"A last minute purchase."

Ah. That makes more sense. Hauling condoms around makes more sense than hauling lube around, but then again, if someone is Devan's size, maybe that's something they need to have on hand. The thought might make me laugh if I wasn't staring so hard at his cock. I swear he's gotten bigger since I had him in my mouth.

He wraps one giant hand around my hip and uses the other to guide his cock to my entrance. "Go slow. You control the pace."

I sink down slowly, stopping when just the head of him is inside me. Part of me wants to rush this, but we're playing a game. "You're too big."

"Getting cold feet, birthday girl?" His grip tightens on my hip and he pulls me another inch down his length. I whimper. Devan works me another inch down his cock. God, he's huge. The fit is uncomfortable, and if I didn't like a little pain with my pleasure, it might be too much. "I should stop," he growls. Another inch. "Tell me to stop."

"Stop," I say immediately. It comes out more like a question.

Devan meets my gaze in the mirror. I can clearly read his expression. *Stop doesn't mean stop. Red means stop.* I give a little nod and he yanks me another inch down his cock. "I can't stop. You feel too good. You can take a little more, can't you?"

"Yes," I sob out.

He keeps working me down his length, one slow inch at a time. His words get rougher with each second that ticks past. "Flaunting this hot little body in front of the entire bar. Practically inviting someone to stick their cock in you. To fuck right there in front of everyone. Would you like that?" He

KATEE ROBERT

grabs my other hip and slams me the rest of the way down, sheathing himself entirely.

I cry out and writhe, though I can't tell if I'm trying to get closer to trying to get away. He's so impossibly deep. It's like his cock is possessing me, marking me as his in way I don't know how to deal with. "No. Just you."

"That's right. Just me." His grip eases a little bit and he skates his hands up my sides to cup my breasts. "It doesn't matter what other cocks you ride, birthday girl. No one is going to fuck you as deep as me. This pussy is mine now. It always will be." He tugs the straps of my swimsuit, loosening them enough to pull my top off, and then repeating the process with my bottoms.

I stare at our reflections. I look exactly like the little slut I feel. Naked against his clothed body. Heat lances me and I relax into it. The fit of him inside me eases a little, edging into pure pleasure. I shiver. "It feels good."

"It's going to feel better." He lifts a hand to press two fingers to my lips. I suck him deep, and his cock pulses inside me. Devan takes his wet fingers and lightly strokes my clit.

He's right. It does feel better.

With every little circle he traces, I lose another layer of coherency. I forget we're playing a game. I forget that this is temporary. I forget everything but reaching the pinnacle. "More." I lean back against his shoulder and focus on riding his cock as much as he'll allow. He keeps me pinned down, keeps himself sheathed to the hilt as he pushes me closer and closer to orgasm. "More," I cry.

"Greedy girl." He releases my hip. "You want more? Take it."

I immediately lean forward and brace myself on his thick thighs. I can't lift myself entirely off his cock, and I have the borderline hysterical thought that he could keep me pinned like this indefinitely. My feet barely touch the ground. All he'd have to do is spread his thighs a little more and I'd be completely at his mercy until his body gives out.

Even the little friction I manage on my own, lifting myself a few inches off him and slamming back down, nearly makes my eyes roll back in my head. "Oh god."

"Not god, Hazel. Me." He keeps up those devastating strokes to my clit, easily matching my pace. "Tell me who this pussy belongs to."

"Devan," I moan. "Yours. It's yours. I'm yours."

"That's right." His voice goes rougher yet. "That's fucking right. Now come all over my cock like the little slut you are."

I keep fucking him as much as I'm able, and he keeps at my clit. I look at myself in the mirror. From this angle, I can't see where we're joined properly, and I suddenly want to. I want to see his massive girth disappear into my pussy. I want to watch my body take him, inch by unending inch. I drag in a breath. "I want you to fuck me again, Devan."

"I'm fucking you right now."

"Again," I repeat. "But I want to film it. Watching is so hot, I want to keep it forever."

He pauses. For one breathless moment, I think I've somehow gone too far, but then Devan bands an arm around my waist and surges up. He was letting me control everything before, but that's over now. He fucks up into me and even with the restricted mobility of this position, I feel entirely owned by him.

I come so hard, I shriek. Devan barely hesitates. He lifts me off him and switches our position, tumbling me onto the couch and kneeling between my thighs. He guides his cock back into me and uses his palms to press my legs up and out, holding me open for him as he fucks me. "This is what you want to see."

I stare down to where we're joined. His cock saws into

me, unbelievably big, my orgasm soaking both of us. "Yes," I gasp. "More."

"So fucking greedy. So demanding. You sure you're a virgin, birthday girl? Because you take this cock like you've done this before." He picks up his pace, borderline pounding into me. "Just. Have. To. Get. Deeper." Devan surges forward and I swear to god I feel him in the back of my throat.

I come again. This time, there's no shriek. I make a choked sound and my body clenches so hard my brain shorts out. He curses and pulls out, jacking his cock in rough, furious movements. On the second stroke, he orgasms, his come lashing my lower stomach and pussy. Devan gives one last stroke and then drags his cock down my slit.

I can't stop shaking. "Holy shit," I whisper. "Holy shit."

Devan's exhale sounds just as shaky as my body. "Yeah." He meets my gaze. "You okay?"

"Okay?" I blink slowly. It feels like my words are being pulled through taffy. "I don't think okay is the word. I think I just had an out-of-body experience."

His expression eases and he shakes his head. "That about sums it up. Don't move."

"Couldn't even if I wanted to."

He leverages himself to his feet, tucks his cock away, and heads in the direction of the bedroom. I lift my head enough to look at myself in the mirror. My body looks as deliciously boneless as I feel, slumped against the couch with my legs spread and Devan's come all over my pussy.

Just…wow.

Am I really going to survive five—no, four—more times of this?

More, how the hell is normal sex supposed to measure up to this? He might have been saying all that in the heat of the moment, driven on by the fantasy, but that doesn't make any of it less true. Devan might really have just ruined me for other partners.

I close my eyes and let my head fall back against the couch. It's too late to worry about it now. If it ends up being the case, then starting tomorrow I'll just do what I've always done.

Pick up all my broken pieces and keep moving.

CHAPTER 10

*D*evan reappears a few minutes later with a warm wet washcloth in his hand. He cleans me up methodically and then gathers me into his arms and resumes his seat with me in his lap. I relax against him and let the beat of his heart soothe me; it draws me back into my body, steady thump by steady thump. I like this nearly as much as the sex, though I'll be damned before I admit it.

"That got a little out of control," Devan finally says.

I lift my head and look at him. "You have a virgin kink. Who knew?"

He holds my gaze. "I'm rapidly coming to realize I have a Hazel kink."

My whole body goes hot and my mind veers into static. "What?" Surely he didn't say what I think he just said. I can*not* handle any non-roleplaying talk that hints at any kind of permanence. When it comes down to it, Devan's only spent a few weeks with me at sixteen that I barely remember and six nights since. If he wanted to be in my life, he would have come around more, at least after my nineteenth birthday.

He didn't.

Tonight is about letting go, not about starting something new. I can't afford to forget that.

In an effort to get us back on track, I wiggle out of Devan's arms and stand slowly. My body still feels a little loose, but I manage to keep my feet without stumbling. "On to twenty."

"Hazel."

I hold up a hand. "Look, if you want to talk about anything that isn't fucking my brains out, do you think it can wait until morning?" His eyes go flinty, but I push on. "I've been fantasizing about this for a really long time, and I don't want something as messy as reality to intrude. Please, Devan."

After a long moment, he nods. "If that's what you want."

"It is." I think. Then again, I thought I had a clear view of what I wanted when I put all this into motion. I didn't expect Devan to lean into the dirtiness of the fantasies and then shove them into an entirely new realm of sexiness. I clear my throat. "I'm going to change."

He watches me for a long moment. "Okay."

I try to tell myself I'm not fleeing the room as I hurry back into the bedroom and grab my bag. Except it *does* feel like fleeing. Like hiding. *What if he wants something more?* I shut that thought down *really* fast. I can't afford to hope. Better to play through this alternate history sequence and leave it at that.

I have to drag a comb through my hair to get out the tangles from Devan's hands, and then I dress quickly. I made a few changes to the costume I wore to the party on my twentieth birthday. It's the same sinfully short pleated plaid skirt and tied-up white top, but I left off the bra and changed out the bikini style panties for a sheer white thong. I've put on some weight in muscle in the last five years, so now the skirt doesn't fully cover my ass and gives taunting peeks to my panties in the front as I move. The shirt is thin enough to see my nipples through. I finish off the look by pulling my hair up into pigtails like I had it that night.

I take a deep breath and head back into the living room. I barely make it two steps through the doorway before Devan grabs me, wrapping a big hand around my forearm and practically carrying me to the small bathroom off the dining room. He shoves me inside and follows me in, slamming the door behind him. "What. The. Fuck?"

I blink as he turns on the light. "Devan? What are you doing here?"

"You don't get to ask questions, birthday girl." He sounds absolutely furious. "Not after you disappeared without a single fucking word to me last year."

Something goes a little funny in my head. Of course we're playing it like this. Of course this alternate history is consistent. Of course I would have snuck off without saying a single fucking word to Devan if he fucked me at nineteen the way he did just a short time ago. "There was nothing to talk about."

"Oh, I think there's plenty to talk about." He leans against the door and crosses his arms over his chest. "Did you put on that slutty outfit hoping I'd show up again this year?"

"Of course not."

"You better be lying." His gaze drags over me slowly, lingering on the top and skirt. "I don't give a damn who you fuck the rest of the year, Hazel. But that pussy is mine on your birthday. So you had better not have been planning to give *my* pussy to one of those frat boys at this party."

My heart speeds up. I lick my lips. "Why stop at one? Maybe I was going to give it to all of them."

I don't know what I expect, but he laughs. The sound isn't

happy, and the hint of cruelty in it makes my thighs clench. "I was going to do right by you."

"Excuse me?"

He continues as if he didn't hear me. "I was going to take you somewhere tonight and give it to you properly. But after that comment, I changed my mind." He pushes off the door. "I'm going to fuck you in this dirty bathroom like the little slut you are. I'm going to make you scream so loud, all those frat boys outside the door can hear you and know you're getting dicked down in a way they couldn't begin to accomplish."

I hold up my hands. "Devan, wait. Let's talk about this."

But he's done talking. Again, I get more than a hint of anger as he crosses the distance between us in one single stride and grabs me. I barely get a squawk out when he lifts me onto the counter and steps between my legs. "Look at that," he murmurs. "Your pussy is there, on display. You really were flashing that invitation at anyone who dared look."

He brushes his fingers along the hem of my skirt where it's fallen up against my waist. "A school girl." His gaze flicks to mine. "Are you trying to remind me that you're my ward?"

"I'm twenty. I'm not your ward."

"You sure as fuck are." He drags his knuckles over my pussy. "I took care of your pussy last year, and I'm going to do the same this year."

"Because you're a good guardian." I manage to inject a thread of sarcasm into my tone, but not nearly enough to combat how needy I sound. "Well then... Do it."

"You are not in charge, Hazel. You want me to stop, I stop, but you don't get to direct this. You want to be in charge? Go fuck one of those frat boys."

I push at his chest. I might as well push at a wall. "I'm *trying* to fuck one of those frat boys."

He hooks his fingers into my panties, rubbing his bare knuckle over my pussy. "You wet for him, birthday girl? That fool who will just jack rabbit into you until he reaches his orgasm, and not worry about figuring out where your clit is actually located?"

Considering the frat boys I've fucked in the past have sex exactly like that, I can't help blushing. "I seem to remember you doing some jack hammering of your own last year."

He keeps rubbing my pussy, his gaze on mine. "And *I* seem to remember you coming around my cock—twice." He reaches into his pocket and my heart dips as I watch him pull out his phone. "You remember what you said last year?"

"Yes," I whisper.

He pulls me off the counter and spins me around. It's low enough that, in my heels, my hips are well above the edge of the counter. Devan reaches around me and sets the phone against the back of the counter, angling it so it shows my hips and upper thighs. He pushes the record button and then reaches between my thighs, roughly palming my pussy. "You miss me, birthday girl?" He lifts my skirt enough to see my panties.

"Of course not." But I'm shaking with the restraint required to hold perfectly still as he touches me, instead of parting my legs further and begging. It's all too easy to imagine I can hear the thumping base on the other side of the door, can hear people partying as Devan slides his big hand into my panties. The image is so hot, I moan a little.

"Maybe you didn't miss me, but this pretty pussy did." He drags a single finger along my slit. Not pushing inside. Just feeling me, testing my wetness. "No one's been taking care of her properly."

"How would you know?"

"You're in this bathroom with me right now, not someone else." He moves his hand out of my panties and tugs them to the side. My pussy is clearly visible on the screen, wet and swollen with desire. Devan parts me. "You haven't told me to stop."

"Stop." I roll my hips to rub myself against his hand. "I don't want you to fuck me in this bathroom. I don't want you to make me come so hard I scream."

"Mmmm. Yeah. I won't do that. I won't do it at all." I feel him sink down behind me, but I can't do anything but stare at the screen of his phone as he tugs my panties down my legs, baring my pussy completely. He guides one leg up to the counter and then his mouth is there, licking me.

I cry out, arching my back to give him better access. The video can't quite see things clearly, but it's obvious his mouth is all over my pussy. It feels so good, the sensation only made better by the fact that this is *wrong*. Devan's tongue slides inside me and I moan. "Oh god, stop. That feels too good."

He speaks against my heated flesh. "Stop riding my face and I'll stop licking this pretty pussy."

I don't stop. I keep rolling my hips, and I can't help but reach down and tangle one hand in his hair. His beard scratches against my inner thighs, and fuck, even that's so hot I can barely stand it. "Oh fuck, oh fuck, oh fuck. I'm going to come." And then I do, orgasming so hard, he has to grab my hips to keep me in place. Devan doesn't stop, though, he keeps eating me out through wave after wave. Too good. It's too fucking good.

Finally, he nips my thigh and then he's climbing back to his feet behind me. A pause and then he's at my back, his cock between my thighs. He leans over my shoulder and looks at the camera. "Look at that. For someone who says she doesn't want this, you come so prettily."

"I didn't have a choice." I shiver at the sight of the length of his giant cock pressed against my pussy. He slides against me, not trying to enter. "It felt too good to stop."

"I'm going to fuck you now, birthday girl."

"We shouldn't."

"Oh yeah?" He wraps a fist around his cock and dips down until he can position the broad head at my entrance. "Is it because you're my ward?"

"No," I whisper. "Not because of that."

"Mmmm." Devan pretends to think as he brushes the head of his cock over me, again and again. My skirt is hiked up just enough to catch some of it in the frame, and there's something about the fact he's going to fuck me with it still on that makes this hotter.

"Oh, I know." He presses into me. In the camera, I watch his cock spread my pussy obscenely. So wide it looks painful, might be painful if we hadn't just been fucking a little while ago, if he hadn't just made me come again. "It's because one of those little frat boys is your boyfriend."

I jolt. "How did you know that?"

"Come on, Hazel." He keeps thrusting slowly, feeding me inch after inch of his cock in the video. "You think I don't keep tabs on you? I know you're dating one of those little shits." He exhales as he sheaths himself completely. "Chad? Brad? One of those frat boy names."

"Jason," I murmur.

"Jason," he repeats. He braces one hand on my hip and starts a slow withdraw. In the camera, his cock is soaked from my pussy. Devan doesn't pull out all the way, just fucks me slowly in short strokes that have his cock brushing against my G-spot. "Does *Jason* make you come as hard as I do?"

"No," I sob out. I'm already close again. I want Devan to finger my clit, but he seems intent on building this orgasm slowly, stroke by stroke.

"Didn't think so." He keeps up that agonizingly good pace.

"You let *Jason* fuck you bare? You let him fill you up with his come?"

"No!"

"That's right. You don't let anyone but me do that, because this is *my* pussy." He grabs the camera and flips it around, pointing it at the bathroom mirror. As I watch, Devan yanks on the tie of my shirt, exposing my breasts. "You're *my* little slut, Hazel. And when I show up, you take my cock like a good little girl, don't you?"

"Yes," I moan.

He finally, *finally* presses his fingers to my clit. "Maybe I should send this video to Jason. Let him know whose pussy he's been borrowing."

I don't think. I just reach behind me to clasp his neck, putting my body even more on display. It feels so fucking good, so fucking wrong. "Your pussy, Devan. It's your pussy."

"Fucking right it's my pussy. Now come for me, birthday girl."

CHAPTER 11

*D*evan circles my clit again and again and then I'm doing exactly as he commands, coming so hard I scream. He shoves the phone into my hand and bends me over the counter. I have just enough control to keep it pointed at the mirror as he grabs my hips and drives into me, so much harder than he did earlier. Deeper. "That's right, Hazel. I'm going to fill you up and I don't give a fuck if you're on birth control because you're going to take it like a good girl."

Holy shit.

"*Yes,*" I moan. "Yes! Do it."

He grinds into me and then he's coming, his expression downright agonized. A few final pumps, and Devan reaches over to turn off the video. This time there's no gentle after-care, though. He picks me up and hauls me out to the main living area where he dumps me on the couch. His cock is still half hard, and he feeds it into my pussy and yanks his shirt over his head. "It's not enough."

His frenzy infects me and I arch up to run my hands up his stomach and chest. "I love what you do to me."

"This shit is fucking with my head." He presses me back down to the couch. "Look at you." He cups my breasts and lightly pinches my nipples. "Tits out and pussy taking my cock so sweetly. I ought to have you like this always. Skirt and no panties. Pussy waiting and ready to go."

I suddenly want that more than anything. "That's so hot."

"Yeah. It is." He keeps fucking me, but it's like my agreement takes some of the ferocity out of him. Devan lifts my hips a little so he hits my G-spot with every stroke. "Fuck, I could stay inside you forever."

I have no response to that because I'm coming again. This orgasm is different from the rest. It feels softer, gentler. The sensation only gets stronger when Devan leans down, pressing his chest to mine, and kisses me. A proper kiss this time, one deep and possessive and the tiniest bit messy. On and on, until we're panting against each other's lips and he tenses and comes again.

Devan presses his forehead to mine. "Fuck."

It takes me two tries to form a response. "That about sums it up."

He moves back and I can't stop a sound of protest. From the look on his face, he feels the same way. I just want to be closer, closer, closer. The last few hours have been beyond anything I've ever experienced. I don't want it to end, even if it's simply a pause while we move from one birthday to the next. Each one takes us closer to the end of this night, to the moment when he pulls out of me for the last time.

What a depressing thought.

Devan gathers me up. I might laugh at his insistence on carrying me around, but honestly I like it. I even liked it on those birthdays when he tossed me over his shoulder and hauled me out of whatever place I was partying at. I'm going to miss this, too.

God, I'm in danger of becoming melancholy.

He carries me into the bedroom and sets me on my feet long enough to divest me of my clothing. His follow, and I don't get an opportunity to ogle him properly because he drags me onto the bed and tucks us in.

I lay half sprawled on his wide chest and try to work up the energy to argue. "We still have three birthdays." Four, technically, but he's right about skipping twenty-two. I don't want to revisit that night. I've never been so grateful for Devan's meddling as I was that night.

He smooths a big hand down the center of my back. "I'm only human, Hazel. You've worn me the fuck out."

I lift my head, something like panic fluttering in my throat. "But if we fall asleep, then it will be morning and this will be over."

Devan takes me in with those dark eyes that have always seen too much. "That bother you?"

"Of course it bothers me." We've already clearly lined out what tonight means, and I'm not about to change the rules now, no matter how my heart aches at the thought of never seeing him again. I can't ask for more. I *won't*. If I dredged up the courage to, and he rejected me, it would hurt too badly. Better to not put myself out there at all, at least not more than I already have tonight.

This paid off. Maybe telling him you want more time would, too?

I ignore that voice. I can't allow hope to kindle, can't indulge it for fear of it being dashed across the rocks of harsh reality.

Devan smooths my hair back. "I'd like to renegotiate."

I blink. Renegotiate?

He keeps going before I can come up with a response. "Another day and night should be plenty of time to hit those last three birthdays."

My chest gets tight. "You're offering another twenty-four hours?"

"Yeah." He watches my face closely. "If you're good with that."

It takes everything I have to keep my expression locked down. Even so, a smile pulls at the edges of my lips. "I suppose I could clear my schedule."

"Do that." He keeps up that soothing touch, trailing his fingers over my temple and down behind my ear. "I think we both need some recovery time."

I'm delightfully sore, but he's right. Much more and that delicious feeling might edge into something uncomfortable. I trail my fingers over the light dusting of hair across his chest. "I guess you'll have to kiss my pussy better before you fuck me again."

He huffs out a laugh. "Don't start something neither one of us can finish."

I'm suddenly afraid that it's exactly what I've done by orchestrating this trip down memory lane for us. How am I supposed to go back to fucking normal people after I've had Devan? He reaches down into my deepest, darkest parts and plucks the strings of my desires there. Without shame. Without judgment.

I don't say any of that aloud, though. There's no point. If I'm gifted with more time with Devan, I won't do anything to endanger it. I have questions for him, though. "Can you answer something for me?"

He tenses, but seems to force himself to relax. "Sure."

"What do you do for a living?"

Devan stares at me for a long moment and then gives a ragged laugh. "What a blow to the ego. You never bothered to look it up?"

"I *did* look it up. You don't have a single social media profile that I can find. You're not even on the business ones."

I honestly considered hiring a private investigator, but even I can recognize that doing so would cross half a dozen lines. Devan never did anything wrong, never acted in any way that would justify invading his privacy. I might be an asshole, but even I have limits. Most of the time.

He settles back against the bed and laces his hands behind his head. "I work in tech security."

"What?" I frown. Of all the things I considered, that had never occurred to me. "You're a geek?"

"Sure, if you want to put it like that. I'm good with computers, better with security systems and building fire-walls and the like." He waves that away. "It's boring shit."

I don't think it's boring at all. I settle more firmly against his side, relishing the closeness even as I tell myself not to get used to it. "I would have thought you'd do something more...physical."

He raises his brows. "What makes you say that? I'm no hard-bodied soldier type. Not anymore."

Not anymore.

He's quiet for a long moment. When he speaks, he guides us back to safer topics. "Why would you think I'm a bruiser?"

"I mean..." I motion at him. "I've never met anyone with such a don't-fuck-with-me vibe. That would be really useful in a number of professions; personal security, corporate security, really any kind of security." Except tech security. I have a hard time imagining Devan behind a screen all day.

I sigh. "I guess it wasn't hard to figure out where I'd gone on my birthdays when you are a tech dude."

"Hazel." He shakes his head slowly. "We talked about this downstairs. You know damn well you wanted me to find you. You tagged your location." He frowns. "You've got to stop doing that shit. It's not safe, especially with all the weirdos who follow you on social media. You're just asking to get tossed into the back of a van."

A thread of warmth curls through me at his ridiculous protectiveness. "I'm safe enough."

"Uh huh." He turns on his side, toppling me off him and onto my back. Sadly, he doesn't immediately take advantage of our new positions; he simply studies my face. "You have some really hardcore fans. It's only sheer luck that one of them haven't edged over into stalking."

Truth be told, there have been some close calls with that sort of thing. Being even remotely famous on the internet paves the way for creepy parasocial relationships that are all in people's heads, and I've gotten my fair share of weird messages and emails and even on one scary occasion, a letter to my home.

Still, I smile because I'm not about to tell Devan that. He might think I'm trying to manipulate his sympathies or invite him to meddle in my life. I am most certainly *not*. "If you're paying that close of attention, you'll realize that these days I only tag a location leading up to my birthday." An invitation of sorts, but only to this man.

"I know." He smiles a little, though it fades nearly as soon as it appears. "Just promise me you won't do it anymore after this birthday."

After this birthday.

After I say goodbye to Devan forever.

CHAPTER 12

I don't mean to fall asleep. When there are so few hours left in this fling, I want to soak up every second with Devan. I can sleep once this is over. Unfortunately, my body has other ideas.

I wake up in a panic, suddenly sure that he's taken this opportunity to slip out of my life permanently. That last night was all a ruse after we came that last time, that he regrets it and just wanted to let me down gently by not letting me down at all. Ghosting is so much simpler than having rough emotional conversations or rejecting the woman who used to be your ward and has a boatload of baggage.

I start to sit up, only to be brought short by a heavy weight over half my body. I open my eyes to find Devan sleeping pressed to my side, one arm draped over my waist and one leg wedged between mine. I couldn't escape this bed if I wanted to, and I suddenly very much do not want to.

He's still here.

There's no point in examining the sheer relief that courses through me at that realization. Certainly no reason to look further into the future to the inevitable crash and burn of my emotions when this is over. I can scream up and down and sideways that this is just sex and just letting off steam that's been building for six years, but some part of me knows it's more than that.

Plenty of time to muddle through that mess later.

I have other things on my mind currently.

Devan shifts against me, hitching his leg higher until his thick thigh is pressed against my pussy. "Morning."

"Morning," I whisper.

"How you feeling with a few hours of sleep behind you?"

Easy enough to read between the lines. He wants to know if I'm having regrets or all freaked out. I *am* freaked out, but not in a way Devan can fix. I squeeze my legs around his, urging him closer yet. "I'm feeling needy."

Devan makes a sound nearly like a growl and buries his face in my neck, kissing and gently biting me. "Can't have that."

"What are you going to do about it?"

"I can think of a few things." He moves down my body slowly, lavishing my breasts with kisses. "A certain birthday girl mentioned kissing her pretty pussy better last night."

I arch up, whimpering as he continues his journey south. "She sounds really smart."

"She is." He settles between my thighs. "Smartest girl I ever met." He kisses my pussy before I can figure out if he's just talking shit or if he actually means it. Devan traces his tongue over me as if he has all the time in the world and intends to taste every inch of me. I melt under his little strokes and licks. Last night was so intense and nearly overwhelming—in a good way—that this slow, lazy moment feels particularly sinful.

I dig my hands into Devan's hair. "More. Make me come."

"When I'm ready." He ignores me trying to tug him up to

focus on my clit. Something about that only makes pleasure weave through me faster. I love that he's so much stronger than me, that he can do anything he wants to me, that he won't unless I want him to. My breathing becomes harsher the closer I get to coming, until I'm panting and whimpering and shaking beneath him.

He shifts up to suck my clit into his mouth—hard—and shoves two fingers into me. I orgasm instantly. Devan doesn't linger this time. He crawls up my body and then he's working his cock inside me in slow, short strokes. I'm still sore from yesterday, but that only makes the pleasure soar higher.

I always did like a little pain with my pleasure.

He doesn't say a word. I don't have the air to try. We simply fuck slowly until he brings me to orgasm again and follows me over the edge. It's only when he drops down next to me that I have the mental capacity to wonder what the fuck just happened. This wasn't a birthday, wasn't any kind of fantasy. This was just us.

Devan looks like he wants to say something, and I'm suddenly certain that he's about to let me down just as gently as the sex we just finished. I can't deal with that. Not right now, when it feels like my heart resides outside my chest, beaten and bloody and far too vulnerable. I react on instinct, slipping out of the bed and fleeing to the bathroom.

Like a coward.

What am I supposed to do?

Tell him that no matter what I said at the beginning, this isn't just sex for me? It might be truth, but the boundaries were very clear when we started this. Devan didn't agree to more, and after everything he's done for me, I'd be the most selfish of bitches to demand it of him. If I was any less selfish, I'd call the whole thing off right now instead of letting it go on and letting myself sink deeper into this murky emotional mess.

I'm not less selfish.

I'm not going to give Devan up a moment before I absolutely have to.

I brush my teeth and wash my face. Without my makeup, I feel naked in a way I didn't even when I didn't have a single item of clothing on. Even pulling on the hotel robe hanging on the back of the door doesn't help. I'm still debating on taking a shower and putting a full face back on when Devan knocks on the bathroom door. "Just a minute," I call. My voice sounds horrifyingly shaky.

"Open the door, Hazel."

"I'm not decent." Why the hell did I say that? It doesn't even make sense.

"Hazel." A pause. "Do you want to use red?"

"No." It's the truth, even if I'm not sure of anything else at the moment.

"Then open this fucking door and stop hiding from me."

Damn him for forcing the issue. He's not being unfair, and that's the worst thing about this. If he was being an asshole I could throw a fit, provoke him into punishing me or something, and we'd be off to the races again. If he was anyone else, it would work. But Devan's not going to be provoked; I know it as soon as I open the door to find him wearing his jeans and nothing else, his arms crossed over his chest and a forbidding expression on his handsome face.

He turns without a single word, but the command is clear enough. I follow him out of the bathroom and through the bedroom, into the main area of the suite. I silently sink into the chair he indicates. I watch with my foolish heart in my throat as he sets a cup of coffee in front of me. It only takes a glance to know it's doctored exactly the way I like it—a drop of cream and too much sugar—but I take a sip to confirm anyway. "How do you know how I take my coffee?"

"Amsterdam. I brought you coffee and breakfast that next morning before I drove you to the airport."

I hold the cup between my hands, letting the warmth soak into my palms. "That was a single time, three years ago. It's such an insignificant detail to remember."

"Nothing about you is insignificant, Hazel." He picks up a second cup and leans against the counter. "Now, tell me why you're freaking out."

"Who said I'm freaking out?" He lifts a brow, and I wilt a little. "I had a plan. It was a very good plan."

Devan takes a drink of his coffee. "I'm not arguing the quality of the plan. Unless I've misread things, we're both enjoying ourselves."

"You haven't misread things." I say it too quickly. God, what is wrong with me? It's been years since I fumbled an interaction this thoroughly. Usually I have no problem keeping my poise and calm, but right now, I feel like I'm about to vibrate right out of my skin and make a run for it. "You haven't misread things," I repeat, slower this time.

He watches me for a long moment. "The morning after the part that's freaking you out?"

"I'm not freaking out."

"Could have fooled me. Normally people who aren't freaking out don't hide in the bathroom and refuse to come out."

He has me there. I take a careful sip of my coffee, mostly to buy time. I don't know what I'm supposed to say. That I am feeling too much and that's why I'm a little freaked out? The man would laugh in my face. "I'm not freaking out," I repeat for the third time. I almost sound like I mean it. "I'm planning for the next birthday."

"Mmmm." Devan sounds like he doesn't believe me,

which is fair. I'm lying through my teeth. He takes another drink of his coffee. "I'm not overly inclined to go hunt down a third person to reenact that."

"You have a problem with sharing?"

He pins me with a look that has my thighs clenching together. "I think we've already established that I don't have a problem with loaning out that pretty pussy if the situation calls for it."

My body warms. "I thought that was all an act."

"Nothing we've done so far is an act, not in the way you mean." He's still looking at me too intensely. "The reason that roleplaying is so hot is that there's an element of truth in it."

I hadn't really thought of it that way, but he's right. We might be exaggerating and playing up certain elements, but there's a reason the core fantasies exist. "Okay, so where does that leave us?" Truth be told, I don't want to invite another person into our little bubble. I have so little time left with Devan, I'm greedy for every second of his attention to be solely focused on me and me alone.

"I have a few ideas."

Anticipation licks through me. Yes, this is better. We've touched on my fantasies. Now it's his turn. More than simple birthday spankings. I want *more*. "Tell me."

He finishes his coffee and sets the mug aside. "I want you to come to me."

I take a large swallow of my coffee. "I'm going to need you to elaborate."

"Every birthday, I've come to you." He pauses, the tiniest indication of nerves, before pressing on. "I want you to come to me, Hazel. I want you to need this cock so bad, you can't stay away. I want you to show up and beg me for it."

The words wash over me in waves. I lick my lips, trying to process. "Yes. I want that, too. All of it."

"You sure?" He's still watching me like I'm a gazelle about

to bolt, like part of him wants to sit me down and crawl around inside my head until he figures out what my earlier issue was. "At some point, we need to have a conversation—"

"I want you to fuck my ass," I blurt. I don't even know if I mean it. The words just pop out in a pure panic because if Devan and I start *talking*, we won't be fucking...maybe not ever again. I want the fantasy he described, but I don't want to *talk*.

He blinks. "No."

"What do you mean, no?"

"Exactly what I said." He pushes off the counter and moves to rinse his mug in the sink. "From your reaction, you've never been with anyone my size, which means you've never been fucked in the ass by anyone my size. That takes time to prep for, otherwise I'll hurt you."

"Maybe I want you to hurt me." Something to remember him by, at least for a little while.

Devan gives me a sharp look. "Not like this, Hazel. You want me to paddle your ass again, we can talk. Other shit is up for negotiation, but I'm not going to do something that will cause you legitimate harm if done improperly."

"I don't care."

"I do." The firmness of his tone says this is one battle I'm going to lose. Damn it. He's probably right, but that doesn't change the disappointment weighing me down. Another experience we won't share because there's just not enough *time*.

I'll just have to make do with what I have. "Fine. Not that. But I want to play out your fantasy."

He looks at me for a long moment and then nods. "Go get ready, then. You want to seduce me, you better look the part."

CHAPTER 13

*J*take my coffee back to the bathroom and start the process of putting myself back together. I stay in the shower far too long, letting the near-scalding water beat away all the mess in my head. By the time I wash my hair and body, I'm feeling almost like myself again. When I turn off the water and step out, I'm not even surprised to find Devan waiting for me.

He watches me dry off, expression nearly as greedy as I feel. Each second that ticks by is another lost. I want more, more, more, to fill up this day with him until there's no room for anything else.

I drop the towel and cross to where he leans against the counter. "See something you like?"

"A mouthy woman who's hell on my self-control."

"I'm sure I have no idea what you're talking about." I catch sight of the lotion bottle in his hands. "I'm more than capable of putting on my own lotion."

"I know." He shrugs. "But I want to do it." Devan levels a serious look at me. "Let me take care of you, Hazel. Even if it's only for today."

How can he say that when he's been taking care of me in his own way for so long? Not like this, of course—not even in person most of the time—but there's no denying that Devan has been looking out for me. He's been a silent presence in my life for so long, one that I've told myself I hated, but have leaned on a little at the same time.

After today, that's gone.

I don't know what to think about that. So I don't think about it at all. "Fine. Suit yourself."

"I plan to." He squirts lotion into his big palm and kneels before me.

It seems unnatural to have this man on his knees in front of me. He's too dominant, too overpowering in a thousand different ways. But here he is, guiding me to put one foot on his knee and rubbing lotion into my skin with the utmost care, as if a rough move might tear me to pieces. It's as agonizing as it is lovely, and I nearly bite my bottom lip bloody as he works his way up my leg to my hip, and then repeats the process with my other leg. No inch of skin is bypassed. Not my hips, my stomach, my breasts. Not my arms and back and ass.

When he finally sits back and looks at me, I'm shaking.

Of course I'm shaking. I always seem to be shaking around this man. The need is simply too much for one body to hold.

"I need you," I whisper.

"You have me."

For now.

The words neither of us speak, but that hang in the air between us all the same. The reminder that this is temporary and was always going to be.

Devan rises slowly to his feet. He's still shirtless, and the casual intimacy of his being partially undressed in front of me is thrilling. He cups my jaw, lightly tracing his thumb over my cheekbone. "I like you like this." Before I can laugh in his face—men always say that and they never really mean it—he continues. "I like the whole smoky eye thing, too." The slightest hesitation, and then his voice deepens. "And you know very damn fucking well that I like your red lips."

"Um."

"Hush. I'm thinking." He finally nods to himself. "I want to make your eyeliner run, birthday girl. Not because you're sad—because you're choking on my cock. First, we eat, then you can come back here and do whatever you want to your face. We'll get started after that."

I want to demand we get started right this second and not waste another minute with something as mundane as food, but from the stubborn set of his jaw, there's no budging him on this. "If you insist."

"I do." He grabs the robe from the hook on the back of the door where I left it and drapes it around my shoulders. Devan drags knuckles over my skin as he closes the robe and knots it.

The damn tease.

I follow him. I'm not even shocked to find a cart with a selection of breakfast items on it, even when Devan pulls off the plate covers to reveal several of my favorites. Pancakes, a veggie omelet, and a mixed berry bowl. He catches me looking and shrugs. "I wasn't sure what you'd like."

I hadn't been able to eat the morning after my twenty-second birthday. It'd felt like the worst hangover of my life, and not even my normal staples had sounded good. Devan had asked me my favorites that morning, too, had ordered them all on the off chance my stomach could handle them. Of course he'd remember them the same way he remembered my preferred way to have coffee.

I go with the omelet and eat slowly, watching him as I do. He's digging his way through a plate of biscuits and sausage gravy that, honestly, looks really amazing. Devan catches me looking and gives a faint smile. "Want some?"

"If you're willing to share."

He grabs a small plate and transfers half a biscuit and plenty of gravy onto it. As he pushes it across the table to me, I'm once again struck by how domestic this is. This is something couples do, right? Share food easily. I can't really remember ever doing it before. I'm a big believer of ordering what you want and sticking with that; if I want fries with my salad, I'll order a side instead of picking them off my partner's plate. Boundaries are important and the last thing I want to deal with is someone's bitching.

I never really stopped to consider that this could be another way of taking care of someone. Maybe it's not with other people, but it feels that way with Devan.

When we finish breakfast, he pours me another mug of coffee, doctors it with a drop of cream and a heaping spoonful of sugar, and sends me to get ready. As I put on my makeup, I allow myself to anticipate what comes next. There's no point in mourning the loss of this man before he's even gone. It means detracting from the pleasure still in my future. I will be totally and completely present during the rest of the day.

I apply my eyeliner a little heavier than normal. Just for Devan.

After the briefest consideration, I decide to put on my spare lingerie set—yes, I brought a spare. A girl can't be too prepared, and I'm glad for that now. It's another garter and stocking set, this time in black. I skip panties entirely. Devan seemed to really like playing with me through the lace last night, but if I was going to seduce, I would do things *my* way. On second thought, I take off the bra, too, leaving only the garter and thigh-highs. A pair of black stilettos completes the image.

I don't have a dress sexy enough for seduction, so I skip it entirely and pull my black coat around me. It's just long enough to cover up the garters, but only barely. Devan's pulled open the curtains in the living room and is sitting at the desk, his gaze on the tablet in his hands. I know he's aware of me, but this is *his* fantasy, and I want to provide it just as perfectly as he did mine.

Taking a deep breath, I rap my knuckles on the door frame. He looks up and surprise flickers over his face. "Hazel?"

"Can I come in?"

"Yeah." He doesn't stand, doesn't move as I approach, his gaze raking over me, taking in the stockings and heel. "Is something wrong?"

"You could say that." I bypass the seating options and don't stop until I'm far too close to be proper. As much as I love submitting to him, there's something thrilling about playing the part of the temptress, especially when I lean back and my coat edges up to reveal the lace tops of my thigh-highs. I worry my bottom lip a little, suddenly nervous despite everything. "Devan, I can't stop thinking about what happened between us."

He carefully sets the tablet aside and appears to give me his full attention. "You shouldn't be here."

"I know."

"If my business partners see—"

"Devan, I *know*." I drag in a rough breath. "It's only been two weeks since I turned twenty. Since we... I... I'm going to break up with my boyfriend."

He narrows his eyes. "Did Chad do something?"

"No, *Jason* didn't do anything. That's the problem." I give a rough laugh. This part skates far too close to the truth, but so has everything else we've done to date. "You made me come more times in that bathroom that he has in our entire relationship. He doesn't care if I get off."

Devan gives me a long look. "Why are you in my office, telling me that you're going to break up with your frat-boy boyfriend? Shouldn't you be telling *him* this?"

"I will." I hesitate. "I just…"

"You just *what?*"

"He didn't even notice. You fucked me in that bathroom and he didn't even notice. He was so drunk, he didn't even smell you on me."

He sits back and crosses his arms over his chest. "Did you fuck him that night, Hazel?"

"No. He wanted to, but… No." It doesn't matter that this is all alternate history. I can *see* it. Jason *had* been so drunk that night that he didn't even notice Devan had shown up and taken me home. He *was* more concerned with coming himself than he ever was with me getting any pleasure out of the whole experience.

"Why are you here?" Devan repeats.

I reach for the front of my coat. I don't have to entirely feign my shaking hands. Button after button, until the coat gapes and he can see exactly how little I'm wearing beneath it. "I'm here because I need you, Devan. I need you to make me feel good again."

"You're here to cheat on your boyfriend." He says it softly, but his gaze is stuck on my breasts. I lean back on the desk and shrug my shoulders so the coat falls off them, giving him a better view.

"Devan." I wait for him to drag his gaze to my face. "How can I cheat on my boyfriend when you were just loaning him my pussy to begin with?"

"Get rid of that coat."

I obey immediately, standing just long enough to toss it aside. The way he looks at me… God, I wish I had a camera to catch his expression right now. Devan looks at me like he wants to memorize this just as much as I do. He nods slowly. "Spread your legs, birthday girl."

This time, I move slower, parting my thighs as he moves the chair closer. He coasts his hands up my legs, pushing them wider yet. "You came into my office in nothing but a coat and tights."

"Yes."

"You trying to get me fired?"

"No." I shake my head. "I just... I wasn't sure you'd want to—"

"Hazel." He cuts through my babbling sharply. "I promised you I'd take care of you, didn't I?" Devan uses his thumbs to part my pussy, his gaze intent. "Obviously I've fucked up if I'm letting some frat boy pound your pussy without getting you off." He glances up. "He ever look at you like this?"

"No," I breathe. "He mostly fucks me at night after a party."

"Fool." He's still watching me as he runs his thumbs over me. "He lick your pussy, Hazel?"

I shake my head. Devan's eyebrows wing up, but he doesn't continue, so I say, "Please. Please make me feel as good as you did before. Please, Devan." His thumb brushes my clit and I jerk. "I need your cock. I need your mouth on me again. I'll do anything."

"Anything?"

I'm already nodding. So easy to promise things when I haven't seen Jason in five years, but I have the sneaking suspicion that I'd agree to this even if I was dating him right now. The rules don't seem to apply to Devan and me. "Yes. Anything."

"I want you to break up with Jason."

I blink. "Well, I was already planning on doing it."

He shakes his head slowly. "I want you to do it properly. Tell him a *man* is seeing to your pussy in a way he never could—the same man who made you come three times in the bathroom of *his* party."

I stare down at him. "I think I'd rather just send him the video you took. Do you still have it?"

"Of course I still have it." He drops his hands and sits back, seeming to be oblivious to the giant cockstand pressing against his jeans. "But I'm not sending it to anyone. Guy like that? He's likely to share it everywhere he can to get revenge on you."

He's not exactly wrong. Jason was a spiteful piece of shit. There's a reason we only dated a few weeks before I dumped him and moved on. Spitefully leaking a sex tape is exactly something he would have done. "It would get the point across."

"I take care of you," Devan says slowly. "That includes this." He pins me with a look that threatens to curl my toes. "Dump him, Hazel. If you do, you can have this cock right now."

"Right now?" I lick my lips. "You promise."

"I'll fuck you on my desk like the little slut you are."

I pull my phone out of the coat pocket and type out a text. Once I'm finished, I flip it around and show Devan. "Good enough for you."

He reads, pauses, and rereads, his eyebrows climbing. "Fuck you, Jason," he reads aloud. "Go fuck yourself, because that's all you're good at. I'm going to go get my pussy taken care of by a man who knows where the clitoris actually is. Lose my number." He sets the phone aside. "That certainly gets the point across."

"I prefer to be blunt."

"I know." He moves quickly, jerking me off the desk and onto his lap, and takes my mouth. It's a searing kiss. Both punishment and reward. Devan grabs my ass and brings me more firmly against him, his cock a hard length against me. But the damned jeans are in the way.

I break the kiss and whimper. "Please. I can't wait any longer."

"Too damn bad. You came here, birthday girl, so you're operating on my timeline. Now be a good girl and get on your knees."

CHAPTER 14

I all but scramble to my knees. Yes, this is what I want. This is everything I want. Devan allows me to undo his pants and draw his cock out, but he looks increasingly irritated as I do. "I can't believe what a little slut you are."

I pause with my hand wrapped around his base. "What?"

"You were going to come in here and fuck me while your boyfriend was back at college." Devan laces his fingers through my hair and guides my head down until his cock presses to my lips. I suck him down eagerly, taking him as deep as I'm able and ignoring the way my jaw almost immediately starts to ache. He holds me there, almost gagging me, and keeps talking. "Look at you. So eager to choke on my cock while you're dating someone little college prick. Good girls don't cheat, Hazel."

I make a sound of protest, but he tightens his grip on my hair. The look on his face is forbidding. "Good girls don't show up at the office of their guardian in only a pair of stockings and heels. They don't sit on their guardian's desk and spread their thighs and beg him to fuck them." His voice lowers, gaining an edge. "Good girls don't do that…but dirty little sluts do."

I moan and suck harder on his cock. I can only bob a little with how he's holding me, but I move as much as I'm able, driven on by his filthy words.

"You're panting so hard for it, you wouldn't stop for anything, would you?" He shakes his head slowly. "I could take a dozen calls, conduct a meeting, and you'd let me do anything I wanted to you."

"*Yes*," I moan around his cock.

"Next time your pussy needs tending to, you come here wearing one of those short little skirts. The ones that flare." He jerks on my hair. "You know what I'm talking about?"

I nod a little. I know exactly what he's talking about.

"Not too short. You have to pretend that you're a good girl, Hazel. If people think you're visiting me so I can fuck you in my office, they'll start to talk. We can't have that." He thrusts a little, and this time I can't help gagging. Devan makes a sound devastatingly close to a growl. "Yeah, come in here in a short little skirt and I'll take off your panties nice and slow. And then you can sit on my lap like a good girl while I run my next meeting. No one will have any idea that my cock is deep inside that needy little pussy of yours, not as long as you don't squirm or moan like you're doing right now. Can you do that for me?"

He pulls me off his cock and I gasp. Tears streak my face and my jaw hurts and I'm so turned on, I might come from this alone. "Yes. I can do that. I can be a good girl."

"Prove it. Go put that skirt on. Right now."

I scramble to obey, nearly tripping over my feet as I hurry out of the room and into the bedroom. I leave panties off again and pull on the skirt from last night. It's not even pretending to be decent, which is honestly perfect. The top is wrinkled all to hell, but I untie it and tuck it in as best I can.

No bra, even though the fabric is still too sheer for anything resembling modesty. I smile a little at myself in the mirror. Good girl? Yeah right.

Devan's idly stroking his cock when I walk back into the room. His mouth turns down when he sees me. "Is this your idea of a joke?"

"What?" I make a show of looking down at myself. "Is something wrong?"

"Get over here."

I walk to him, loving the way he drinks in the sight of me, his hand moving faster on his cock. Yeah, he likes what he sees, all right. He shakes his head. "Hands on the desk."

I move quickly to do as he commands, though I bend over a little more than strictly necessary, biting back a smile at his curse. "Are you sure nothing's wrong, Devan?"

"I ought to paddle your ass for showing up here in that little cock-tease of a skirt," he mutters. He doesn't give me time to brace. He simply pulls me back onto his lap and then his cock is there, shoving deep so fast that I cry out.

"None of that. You knew this would happen the second you waltzed in here in *that* skirt." Devan plants a hand over my mouth even as he pulls me the rest of the way down his length. "You have to be quiet, birthday girl. They can't know I'm balls deep in this tight little pussy. It might give someone the wrong idea." His hand flexes against my mouth. "Can you be quiet?"

I nod, even though I'm not entirely sure. We're not in an office, but I can picture it so clearly. Can pretend we're not alone, that no one is supposed to know we're fucking while he's at work. "I can be quiet," I whisper.

"We'll see."

"Why are you so mad?" I'm not fighting to keep a smile from my face now. I'm too focused on not moaning at the feel of him inside me. "I did what you asked."

"No, you didn't. I *asked* you to come in here dressed like a good girl." Devan spins the chair, facing the large mirror. "Do you *look* like a good girl right now?"

Not even a little bit. My shirt clearly shows my nipples and my skirt barely covers my pussy. "Yes?"

"No." He cups my breasts in rough hands, plucking at my nipples through my shirt. "Keep your legs closed, little slut. Don't want anyone to see up your skirt."

I press them close together, and we both pause as it makes me clench tighter around his cock. "Devan," I gasp.

"Hush. You promised you'd be quiet." He keeps playing with my breasts. If not for the color high in his cheeks and his hard cock inside me, I'd think he's just as unaffected as his expression claims.

"I'm trying." I squirm on his lap, squirm around his cock. It feels so good, I keep doing it. "I missed you so much. I thought I could hold out until my next birthday, but I needed you." True, true, true. Except it's present tense. I *need* him. I'm in over my head and sinking fast. Every fantasy only blurs the lines a little more, only drags me down deeper.

"You're about to get me fired," he mutters as he unbuttons my top and yanks it open. Devan turns the chair back to the desk. "Pussy too good to resist." He lifts me off him, spins me around, and all but shoves me back onto the desk. And then his mouth is there, eating me out messily as I cling to the desk and try to be quiet.

"Don't stop," I moan.

He doesn't. He keeps licking and sucking until I come. And I'm not quiet when I do. Devan lifts his head and glares. "You're so goddamned disobedient."

"Sorry."

"No, you're not." He stands and then he's feeding his cock into me. This time, there's no playing around, no teasing. He fucks me roughly, one pounding stroke after another, planting a hand on my hip and shoulder to hold me in place.

I love every second of it.

It feels dirty in an entirely different way than everything else we've done so far. He made me orgasm and now he's using my body for his own pleasure. Devan's strokes lose their smooth rhythm and he curses, and then he's coming, fucking me even harder as he finishes inside me. He moves his hands to the desk and drops his head to my shoulder. "Well, fuck."

"You keep saying that," I gasp.

"Can't help it." He turns his face to my throat and presses a kiss there. "Too rough?"

I shake my head. "No."

"Good." He gathers me up and heads into the bedroom. "I think we've both earned a nap before the next round."

I smile against his shoulder. I'm delightfully sore, and I know if I start thinking too hard about how few hours we have left, I might freak out a little bit, but I'm not going to turn down being close to him for a little bit. "Did I wear you out, old man?"

Devan snorts. "More like you're going to be sporting an array of aches and pains tomorrow and I'm trying to alleviate some of them."

Tomorrow.

When this is over.

Damn it.

As he strips us out of our remaining clothing, I can't help the sinking sensation of seconds ticking away, slipping through my fingers no matter how hard I try to grasp them. Devan climbs into the bed and I join him, pressing hard against his body. He wraps his arms around me and it feels so perfect, I have the horrible feeling like I might cry.

I wish it wasn't perfect.

I wish he balked at something I suggested, or talked down to me, or was actually an asshole, or *anything* that would be an excellent reason to be relieved he's out of my life. Instead, every moment feels like a gift that I'll cherish forever.

It's going to hurt so much when this is over.

CHAPTER 15

*A*fter a power nap I didn't mean to take, it's time for another clothing change. At this rate, I'm going to be wearing my coat and nothing else home, but it's more than worth it. I pull on the bra and panties I skipped the last time we fucked and head back into the bedroom. Devan's sitting on the edge of the bed, waiting for me, and the look on his face when he registers what I'm wearing is more than reward enough for the clothing choice.

"Look at you, all dressed up, just for me."

"Do you like it?" I do a slow spin. Obviously he does, but my heart still lodges in my throat while I wait for his answer.

Finally, Devan leans forward and props his elbows on his knees. "You trying to provoke me, birthday girl?"

I have to fight to keep from squirming. This is what I need; to focus on the here and now and not what comes later. This man can keep me grounded…at least until it's time to let me go forever. I try for a smile. "Maybe a little."

"Though so." He motions me closer. "Get over here and let me look at you properly."

I cross to him on suddenly unsteady legs and set my hand

in his. Devan tugs me closer yet, situating me between his thighs. He eyes me. "This shit is expensive."

"It's designer. One of a kind, and custom made for me."

"Bill me."

I barely register the words before he takes the lace edge of my bra and rips the cup completely off. I stare in shock. "What are you doing?"

"I like the framework. Don't like you hiding from me." He repeats the process with the second one. Without the cups, my breasts are still lifted up by the underwire a bit, but completely exposed. He sets his teeth into the curve of my left breast. "Better."

"Devan—" I have to swallow hard and try again. "Devan, this bra costs an absurd amount of money. I've never even worn it before."

"Bill me," he repeats.

While I'm still processing what just happened, he reaches between my thighs and palms my pussy. "I won't lie, I like touching you like this. Like the thought of you in a short little skirt with these tease of panties on, just waiting for my hand to make you feel good." He tugs the fabric to the side. "I like thinking about doing this while we're out to brunch. No one has to know that I've got two fingers deep inside you while you're eating those pancakes you like so much. No one has to know that you're about to come all over my palm as you drink one of those fucking fruity brunch drinks."

"Mimosas," I gasp.

"Yeah. Mimosas."

I weave on my feet and have to grab his shoulders. I like what he's describing. I crave it. It's really too damn bad it's never going to happen. "I think you have a panty fetish."

"Only for you." He hooks his fingers around the center of them and tugs them down my thighs. "But I want unfettered access to your sweet pussy for the rest of the evening, so these have to go."

"I'm not going to argue with that."

"Good, because you don't have a choice." He finishes removing my panties and slides them into his pocket. "I'm keeping these."

"Like I said—panty fetish." Something strange and uncomfortable takes up residence in my throat. Something that feels a whole lot like jealousy. "I bet you have a whole drawer of them back at your place."

Devan leans back and looks at me. I can't read the expression on his face. "That street goes both ways. You're just packing a spare set of designer lingerie around?" He shakes his head. "Seems like you were planning to leave this hotel room and jump right into bed with your next partner."

I don't know if we're playing or not. I honestly can't tell. This feels all too real in a way that I don't know how to deal with. Is he jealous of the thought of me with other people? Or is he just playing into what he thinks is a fantasy? If I was braver, I'd ask.

I'm not brave. No matter what I project to the world, I'm a fucking coward at heart.

"And what if I am?" The words are out before I can think better of them or call them back. I've gone too far to change my mind now. I'm too stubborn to admit I don't know if I want to go down this path. The other fantasies were close to the truth, yes, but those events already happened differently. Rewriting them is safe, in a way. The stakes are so much lower.

Playing out a fantasy set in the here and now?

That's something else altogether.

Maybe we should just stick to the birthday plan. I have the body paint ready to go. It would be so much safer to put on the brakes and guide us back to those scenarios.

Devan runs his knuckles up and down my hips before I can decide if I want to suggest it. "What if you're planning on leaving this hotel room and jumping into bed with someone else."

It's not quite a question, but I nod. "Yes. What then?"

He frowns, a tightness working its way into his jaw and shoulders. Those dark eyes search my face, and I have the uncomfortable feeling that he's seeing right through me. Finally, he shakes his head slowly. "You're taunting me."

"Doesn't mean it's not true."

God, why did I say that?

Why can't I keep from snapping at him like a creature with its leg caught in a trap? We only have so much time. Surely I can keep myself from ruining it? I have to.

"You're taunting me," he repeats. He takes my hips, the tiniest of pressures that brings me closer, inch by inch, until I'm straddling one of his big thighs. His slow smile has a cruel edge that makes things low in my stomach clench. "You want me to fly into a jealous rage, toss you on that bed, and fuck you while telling you that no other cock will make you feel like I do."

I open my mouth, but nothing comes out. It takes swallowing hard before I'm able to speak. "You've already said that earlier. That no other cock will compare."

"Earlier was different and you know it."

I do know it. I was just thinking the same thing, after all.

Devan smooths his hands over my hips. "That's not the problem though, is it?" He doesn't give me a chance to respond, just keeps digging around inside my chest with his words. "You don't like the thought of me with other people. Quite hypocritical of you, birthday girl."

"I don't care what you do," I lie. "Fuck your way through New York City if you feel like it. That's your prerogative."

"So proud." He leans forward and trails light kisses along

my lower stomach. "So fucking proud. You ever get tired of standing on that pedestal you created, Hazel? Of being unfuckingtouchable?"

"No." Another lie.

"Liar." This time, it sounds like a challenge. "You think I won't drag you off the damn thing and down with the rest of us? Silly girl. It's long past time for someone to put you in your place."

I recognize that Devan is moving us back to safer territory, but part of me wants to dig in my heels out of spite. The thought of him with others stings, a slashing cut that I didn't even feel at first, but now consumes me. "Pull me down from my pedestal, put me in my place, and then move on to the next princess to tarnish."

Devan narrows his eyes. "You're hung up on the thought of me with someone else. Something you want to say, Hazel? Stop choking on it and spit it out." When I don't immediately respond, he releases me and drapes his arms over the back of the chair. "What do you care if I grab a pretty partner or two and fuck away every memory of you after this? You have a use for me, but it's temporary. You've been damned clear about that."

"I—"

"You get this cock tonight." He palms himself through his jeans. "You want to renegotiate, that's a different conversation."

Of course I want to renegotiate. One night was never going to be enough, two nights certainly isn't. Devan and I have shown each other our sharp edges; have realized that, at least where fucking is concerned, those edges come together to create a puzzle that I could spend years exploring. We *fit*.

But that might be all in my head.

Poor little rich girl, throwing herself at the one person in her life who's been entirely consistent, if distant. That distance is almost an asset. It sets me up to throw myself against him safely without actual consequences. Or it did, until last night. Until I crossed every line with him. Until he reached into my chest and touched me in places no one else has.

That's the problem.

More sex won't change anything. It will probably make this feeling worse. Renegotiating just means falling harder for Devan while we fuck over a prolonged period of time, and if two days is enough to mess me up like this, I don't know if I'll survive longer. It will hurt too much.

"I don't want to renegotiate," I manage.

I must be imagining the disappointment that flickers over his face. He shrugs. "Then my question stands—what do you care?"

"I don't."

Devan tenses and then seems to make himself relax. "Lie to yourself if you want to, Hazel, but don't lie to me. You don't like the thought of me fucking others." He moves quickly, snaking an arm around my waist and pulling me down to straddle his lap. "Just like it makes me fucking *feral* to think about you with other people."

I don't mean to sink my hands into his hair. I sure as hell don't mean to tug sharply on it. "Not too long ago, you were saying you don't mind sharing."

"I don't." Devan's not passive. His body is all coiled strength waiting to spring into motion, but he allows me to tilt his head back so I can meet his gaze. The possessive look there scalds me. He tightens his grip on my hips and jerks me closer, pinning our hips together. "Sharing means you're mine, Hazel. It means that pussy belongs to me, and if you want a threesome or an orgy or whatever the fuck you can dream up, that's something *I'm* giving to you. It doesn't matter if it's not my hands, cock, mouth that's delivering it.

107

It's still at my will. You're a smart girl. You understand the difference."

I do.

I don't have a clever answer to that, though, so I kiss him. It's a fierce meeting of mouths, almost a battle. Devan kisses me like he knows I'm keeping things locked up tight and he's sure he can steal the words right off my tongue.

Suddenly I'm all to happy to give him words. Not all of them. But ones I most certainly shouldn't voice. I break the kiss and grab the hem of his shirt. He allows me to pull it over his head, but when I see his face again, it's all challenge. "You have something to say, birthday girl?"

Even as I tell myself to play it cool, to not give him more than I already have, I grab his hand and guide him to press it to the apex of my thighs. "Have fun with your little friends, Devan. Do you claim their pussies and cocks the way you claim me?"

"No," he grinds out. "You get special treatment."

My heart trills even as it breaks a little bit more. "That's because I'm special. We're special." I roll my hips, grinding myself against his palm. "You can fuck as many people as you want. It's not going to change the fact that you'll be thinking about *my* pussy until you're old and gray."

My words snap whatever leash has been holding him back. Devan digs his hand into my hair and bends me backward until I'm relying on his strength to keep me off the floor. "You think your pussy is that good? So good I'll be comparing every other person to it for the rest of my fucking life?"

I can't breathe, can't think. Can only speak the truth. "Yes."

He curses. "You're goddamned right it is." He kisses my breasts roughly, almost like he's marking his territory. Maybe I shouldn't be into that, but I most definitely am. I want him to touch me harder than he did with the spanking last night. To leave little marks on my body that I'll be wearing for days. Something more permanent than we are.

More, more, more.

I need endlessly more.

He lifts me easily and carries me to the bed, dropping down on his back. I try to find my balance, but Devan doesn't give me a chance. He lifts me up to straddle his face. And then his mouth is on my pussy and, *fuck*, I'm going to miss this so fucking much. The way his tongue plays over my most intimate flesh, how he knows exactly how to torment me with pleasure. How *dirty* it feels when he slides his tongue into me while he watches my face.

"Yes," I moan. I rock my hips and he lets me rub myself on his lips and tongue, moving in time with me in a way designed to get me off hard and fast. I try to slow down, wanting this to last, but he grabs my hips, forcing me to keep pace. All too soon, my entire body clenches and I cry out as I come all over him.

He slides out from beneath me and I slump to the bed. I manage to turn my head to watch him take off his pants. This is all moving too quickly, a frenzy driven by the sheer lack of time we have left. Even so, I can't help appreciating the sight of him. "You should be naked more often," I murmur.

Devan hesitates. "You like what you see."

"No shit I like what I see." I push myself up so I can view his whole body. God, he's just perfect. Soft and hard and so damn strong. I lick my lips. "I can't decide what I want to take a bite out of first—your thighs or your chest."

"Dirty girl," he murmurs, but his lips curve a little. "Get on your hands and knees for me."

I obey slowly, liking how closely he watches me. Devan finally crawls onto the bed behind me and runs his hands over my back and hips, down to grip my thighs. He spreads me even wider. "Better."

It's so much easier like this. He's owning me, but without his dark gaze seeing too much, I'm able to say. "Mark me."

He pauses. "Mark you."

"Yes."

Devan dips his thumbs down to part my pussy. He shifts and then the blunt head of his cock is there, pressing against me. "Elaborate."

I drag in a breath, but he doesn't push inside, doesn't move except a slight flexing of his hands against the lower curve of my ass. I've already told him what I want; it isn't so hard to give him the clarification he needs. "I want bruises from your fingertips. I want to keep a part of you."

"Even bruises fade eventually, birthday girl. Nothing lasts forever. Not even this."

Especially not this.

CHAPTER 16

*W*e've already extended our time once. It won't happen again. Devan knows it, and I know it. I close my eyes, hating the gritty feeling of unshed tears. "Still. That's what I want." *Mark me so I have a piece of you past this deadline. Please.*

He hesitates so long, I suddenly wish I could see his face, even though I know I won't be able to identify any of the emotions he's actually feeling. He's too good at keeping things locked down. Finally, Devan moves, thrusting into me slowly. Every other time we've done this, he's worked himself into me in slow strokes.

Not this time.

He's not moving fast, but he's also not giving me time to adjust. I whimper and jerk forward, trying to escape the endless onslaught of his giant cock, but he tightens his grip on my hips, pinning me in place. Each fingertip digs deliciously into my skin, a constellation of pain on each hip. I know even without looking that I'll sport his bruises later. Maybe not forever, but for a while. For longer than a moment.

Even still, it's almost too much. I feel like he's breaking me down, shattering my already jagged edges. "Wait!"

Devan hesitates. "Wait doesn't mean red." But he waits all the same.

"I know." A tear escapes the corner of my eye, and then another. I can't stop them. I don't even bother to try. At least he can't see my face, won't know...

I really should stop under-estimating this man.

He pulls out of me and flips me onto my back. Devan takes in my tears in and gently reaches out and brushes his thumb over the sensitive skin beneath first one eye and then the other. "Do you want me to stop?"

"No." I shake my head. I can't stop the tears, can't explain to him that this is good and bad and inevitable, all at the same time, all tangled up inside me. "No, I don't want to stop. Please."

For a moment, I think he might ignore my words, bundle me up, and do something horrifying like take care of me. I like being held by Devan almost as much as I like fucking Devan. There's something about being wrapped in his arms that makes me feel like nothing in this world can touch me, that he'll step between me and whatever tries to hurt me.

I can't accept that right now.

It will hurt even more than anything he can do to my body, because it's *not real*. This is only temporary, which means no matter how kindly or harshly he treats me, it's all part of one fantasy or another.

I can't let it be real.

I wrap my hands around his wrists. "Fuck me, Devan. Fuck me hard. Please."

He studies my face for a long moment, dark gaze touching on my eyes, the tear tracts down my cheeks, my mouth that feels ravished after our earlier kisses. Finally he shakes his head. "No."

"But—"

"That's not what you need, Hazel."

"You don't get to tell me what I need!"

His lifts his brows, but his face is oh-so-serious. "Don't I?"

"No." I start to sit up, but he plants a big hand in the center of my chest and pushes me back down. I glare. "Let me go."

"Do you want to use red?"

God, I've never hated a man the way I do in this moment. Of course I don't want to use red. We're so close to the end of this thing, using red now might *actually* end it, and that's something I can't live with. "No."

He doesn't mock me for my submission. He just hooks one arm under my thigh and spreads me wide so he can start working his cock into me again. "You don't need to be fucked, Hazel."

I'm so furious and hurt and turned on, I can't keep my mouth shut. "Oh, sure, keep pretending you know what I need."

"Don't have to pretend." He thrusts forward a little more, finally sheathing himself entirely within me. He braces himself on his elbows and holds my gaze. "I know what you need. I've always known what you need."

"And, pray tell, what's that?"

"Someone to take care of you." He kisses my neck as he starts moving slowly within me. "Someone to tell when you've been a dirty little slut and need the attitude fucked right out of you. Someone to be a safe place for you, a harbor in the storm." He starts moving slightly faster, pleasure over-taking his words, to the point where I'm certain I don't hear the next bit correctly.

I couldn't have possibly. Because I could swear he said… "Someone like me."

Devan's dick is too good. It has me hallucinating feelings.

Except I know that's not the truth, it's never been the truth. I drag my hands down his back to grab his ass, urging him to thrust deeper, harder, even if he never increases the pace. It feels too perfect to be held by him like this, fucked by him like this. Like it's not fucking at all, but something entirely more emotional.

Even though I know better, I can't help striking back with the only weapon I have. My words. "You don't know *me*, Devan. You never have."

"Wrong." He wedges one arm beneath my hips, lifting them into an angle that lets him go deeper yet. "I know you in every stubborn, glorious detail."

Now it's my turn to throw his accusation back in his face. "Liar."

"You were right before." His voice has gone rough as he fucks me. "Not the little details. Not the bullshit. But I know *you*, Hazel Gardner, and don't try to tell me otherwise." And then his mouth is on mine again. This time, he doesn't back off. Devan fucks me like he's mad at me, like if he can just make me come hard enough, he can convey some understanding to me that's slipping through my fingers.

I want that understanding just as much as I'm scared of it. It doesn't matter what fantasies we weave here, because they're *fantasies*.

What he's saying sounds so much closer to the truth.

I know better than anyone that sometimes the truth hurts. Hurts so bad, you can't breathe past it, until all that's left are pained animal noises emerging from your throat.

"Hazel."

I blink up at Devan. He's frowning. "Where'd you go?"

"Nowhere."

"Liar. You want distance, and that's bullshit." He hooks my right leg over his arm and presses it up, allowing him to sink even deeper. Devastatingly deep. "You want to pretend you're not undone by me, birthday girl? Not fucking likely."

"Shut up." I grab his hair and tug him back down to my mouth. The kiss is fierce and far too short. And then he's *looking* at me. God, the man is always looking at me. Always seeing too much. Always delving right down to the heart of me.

I shove at his chest, and he lets me move him back. I whimper a little as his cock leaves my body, but the temporary loss is better than having him read me like a book. I flip over onto my stomach. "Like this."

For a moment, I think he won't keep fucking me, but he gives a ragged laugh and presses a hand to the middle of my back, pushing me down so my ass is in the air. "It's like that, is it?"

"I don't know what you're talking about."

"Liar. Always such a fucking liar with that pretty mouth, spouting bullshit." He all but shoves his cock into me, resuming his grip on my hips from before. But harder. So much harder. "Do you believe the lies you tell, birthday girl?" He thrusts forward and drags me back at the same time, sinking impossibly deep.

So fucking deep. Deeper than anyone's gone before.

He really has ruined me.

It makes me want to return the favor.

I brace my hands against the headboard as he fucks me roughly. It *is* fucking now. There's no softness left in Devan, and I relish the sound of flesh meeting flesh that fills the room. "I'm not the only liar in this room."

"Mmmm." He lifts my hips a little higher and does something different with his stroke that has my eyes damn near rolling back in my head. Devan, the bastard, knows it. He gives low laugh. "Say it again and mean it."

"Liar," I gasp. "Pretending you haven't wanted me this entire time. Pretending you're better than the horny feral creatures we both are."

He does that motion again, but he tightens his grip on me to the point where I dazedly wonder if maybe I really will be wearing his marks forever. "You. Were. My. Ward." Each word a devastating stroke.

"Liar," I repeat. "Not after I turned eighteen."

Devan pauses for a long moment and then he releases my hips. One hand lands next to my head and the other snakes around to stroke my clit. The new position has his chest against my back, his lips at my ear. "You're so full of shit," he growls, even as he works my body closer to orgasm, even as he keeps fucking me. "You were still a traumatized teenager at nineteen. I would have had to be a monster to touch you."

"You wanted to."

"Fuck yes, I wanted to." He bites the back of my neck, hard enough to make me gasp. "But even I have lines, Hazel."

I want to... I don't even know. Throw myself against the massive wall that is his control. He might be here with me right now, but he's never going to step out of line with his plans. There's no room for a future between us; Devan has all but said as much multiple times since the beginning of this. Fucking him was never meant to be the start of something.

It's an ending.

I just didn't expect it to hurt so much.

His wicked fingers keep stroking me even as he slows down, once again working me just the way I need to get off. I try to fight it. Of course I try to fight it. Each orgasm moves us closer and closer to the final one. To goodbye.

My body doesn't care. I come hard, sobbing into the sheets. Devan doesn't stop. He doesn't even slow down. He keeps fucking me, dragging my body into another wave of orgasm, stronger this time. My brain shorts out. That's the only excuse I have for the words that slip free. "I love you."

Devan's stroke hitches, and for one horrible moment, I think he's going to stop. To pull out of me, sit me down, and explain that this just sex and no, silly girl, he doesn't really care for me beyond the history we have. It's *history* for a reason.

But then he starts moving again. He presses a kiss to the spot at the back of my neck where he bit me and then moves back, urging my hips high again. I mourn the loss of him, even as I go molten at the delicious angle.

Oh fuck, I'm going to come again.

I feel the words bubbling up a second time, just as unforgivable as the last. Instead, I press my face to the mattress as I come so hard I scream into the mattress. Devan follows me over this edge this time, grinding deep and cursing as he comes inside me.

He rolls us onto our sides and wraps his arms around me, his cock still lodged deep in my pussy. I blink too rapidly, determined not to let the burning in my eyes become something more. Not again.

I wait for Devan to say something, to comment on the unforgivable words I let slip, but he seems content to merely hold me close and trail kisses over my shoulder and neck. I don't know if that's better than addressing it or worse. I'm too tired to figure it out.

Besides, it feels good be held by him. Almost as if he cares just as much as I do, as if his foolish heart has betrayed him the same way mine has. I know it's a lie. Devan would never lose control enough to catch feelings for a woman he's glad to finally be rid of. An albatross at his neck he's finally putting down.

He'd have to be a fool to pick me back up again at this point.

I close my eyes and focus on getting myself under control. An impossible task. I'm one giant exposed nerve for this man. He might call me a liar, but I'm far too honest for both our sakes.

This time, when sleep takes me, I welcome it.

CHAPTER 17

*J*wake up to the light filtering through the hotel room window. I wish I had magic powers to banish the sun from existence, to reverse its path and keep the moon residing in the sky for another hundred hours. It wouldn't be enough. I can recognize that now, even if I couldn't a few days ago. I crave this man on a level I thought I understood. Silly, silly woman.

I knew nothing.

Devan looks so fucking peaceful when he sleeps. He's stretched out on his back, one arm flung over his eyes. It's the first time he's stopped touching me since we got into bed, and that absence is what woke me. I reach out a hand, but stop before I make contact with his chest. What will it accomplish? I'm just going to prolong the moment of good-bye. Worse, he's already proven that he's very intuitive when it comes to my needs.

I want something he can't give me, and that will hurt him and make him uncomfortable, which will just make this situation that much more unbearable. He'll try to let me down gently. I know myself well enough to know that I'll respond by striking out, and that will ruin all the good memories we just created.

No, there's only one thing to do.

I slip out of bed and dress quickly, pulling on a pair of jeans and a top that I had packed for the morning after. Scraps of my lingerie are tossed around the room, but I don't want to gather them all up; every moment I linger is one where Devan might wake and demand to know what I'm doing.

Instead, I detour into the bathroom, shove all my stuff into my bag and head for the bedroom door. I pause there and look back. Devan hasn't moved, aside from the steady rise and fall of his chest.

He opens his eyes and looks at me.

I freeze.

There's no denying exactly what I'm in the process of doing—sneaking out without saying a word to him. Being a coward of the highest order. I hold my breath, waiting for him to ask me where I'm going, or maybe tell me to get my ass back to bed. Devan does neither of those things.

He shuts his eyes.

Loss reaches up and slaps me in the face. I suspected my feelings were one-sided, but this just confirms it. He doesn't want a messy ending, either. He'd rather I slip out of his life, never to be seen again, than to awkwardly let me down easy. That's a good thing. That's what I wanted.

So why does it feel like someone wrapped their fist around my throat and is squeezing for everything they're worth?

Numb, I turn and stumble down the hallway. I stop in front of the desk with the hotel stationary on it, but what could I possibly write that wouldn't come off as either begging him for more or shitting on what we've shared?

Except... Did we really share anything at all if *this* is how it ends?

This is what I wanted.

Maybe, one day, I'll actually believe it.

Besides, it's better for both of us if Devan never knows that I feel like I left my heart back in that bedroom with him. He's too strangely honorable; if he knew, he might try to make things work just to avoid hurting me. I don't want that. I want to be with someone who *chooses* me. Not someone who is only in my life because they were thrust there by my parents' death.

Leaving this hotel suite shouldn't be one of the hardest things I've ever done.

And yet...

By the time I make it to the street and flag down a cab, my chest feels like I've strapped a boulder to it. Too heavy, too tight. Everything hurts in a way that has nothing to do with what Devan did to me last night.

It doesn't matter. All pain fades with time. Even this. Maybe especially this.

I just need to get my head on straight and realize that I didn't really fall in love with Devan McGuire. Time will help gain perspective; I'm sure of that. But I don't want to wait, so I'll just have to go to the next best thing. Distance.

I stop by my apartment long enough to shower, change, and pack a small bag. I flip through my passport, looking at all the stamps from so many different countries. Surely the solution to these horrible feelings inside me lay in one of them.

But first, I have a stop to make.

Two weeks and three countries later, I have to admit I miscalculated. Nothing helps. Not the cold, not the sun, not the gorgeous locales that have always soothed me in the past. Certainly not the lingering constellation of faint pain on my hips. I don't even feel like taking pictures for my social media, and I had so many comments asking where I was and if I was okay, I had to write a freaking statement in the notes app and let everyone know I'm taking a short hiatus.

In short, I'm miserable.

How the hell does the loss of a man who wasn't even in my life to begin with hurt so much? I never realized how much I felt Devan's silent presence, even if I only saw him one night a year. There was just this belief that if I ever really needed him, he'd be there. I might have learned to fight my own battles, to banish my army of personal demons, but in the moments when my resolve wobbled, Devan was there to ensure no harm came to me.

I don't have that strange sort of safety net anymore.

Turning twenty-six is going to be a nightmare.

I close my eyes and lean back against the lounge chair. The gentle sound of the waves do nothing to calm me, even though the sun, sand, and ocean have been a foolproof mood-boost every other time in the past.

Without thinking about it, I pick up my phone and check my email. And there it is, right at the top. An email from my attorney letting me know that the trust fund is officially under my control and suggesting we make an appointment to go over everything as soon as possible.

It's over.

"Of course it's over." I almost delete the email, but that's as childish as hiding under the covers and hoping a thin sheet is enough to protect you from the monsters in the dark. The real world doesn't care about your fears or hurts. It kicks you in the teeth and then carries on, dragging you behind it whether you're ready to move on or not. Clinging to the past won't accomplish a single damn thing but making everything hurt more.

I scroll through my email. There's one from my therapist, gently checking in after my birthday. I respond to that one, letting her know I'm doing okay and rescheduling my appointment for this week. Again.

I'm not ready to go back to New York.

Which means I need to book a flight. Running never helped me solve anything; something I should have remembered before I ran from Devan that morning. The more time and distance I get from it, the more I wonder if I misread the entire moment. Yes, he didn't call me back or chase me, but from the comments he made, he's already very aware of what he perceives as a power imbalance between us. He might not be my guardian anymore, might not be the executor of my trust, but maybe those factors came into his decision to let me go. Maybe he was trying to respect *my* decision.

Damn it, this is a mess. I'll never know because I don't even know where Devan lives. I have his phone number, but it feels very uncomfortable to text him something like *hey, I know I took off like a thief in the night after we hooked up, but maybe we should talk more?*

I...can't.

I put myself out there seducing him. I did it again when I confessed my fantasies about my birthdays, and *again* when I slipped up and told him how I felt. He pretended he didn't hear me, but I know he did.

Maybe it's foolish to let my pride draw this line in the sand, but I can't shake the feeling that if I chase him down now, if we fall into something more long-term, I'll always wonder if he's only capitulating because he doesn't want to hurt me. That fear might be foolish in the extreme, but I can't shake it.

No, if Devan wants me, I need him to chase me. Just a little.

I switch over to my social media and scroll for a bit. Beautiful images of beautiful people, most of them as carefully curated as my social media feed. I see that a friend tagged her location, and that makes me think of Devan and his insistence that I stop doing exactly that. I sigh and keep scrolling. *Everything* makes me think of him these days. It's something I'm going to have to make my peace with, apparently. Having a broken heart might make for some amazing creative projects for artists, but it's highly overrated for normal people.

I sit up abruptly. Wait a damn minute. What if I…

It feels like such a long shot, but I don't care. Anything is better than sitting here and wondering if I fucked things up. At least this way, I'll know for sure if he's not interested in seeing me again. It will provide some much-needed closure. Then I can truly move on.

Hopefully.

It takes too much to go back to my hotel room and make myself photo ready, but I have a brand to consider and I don't want any part of this to be in half-measures. When I'm ready, my hair in waves, some lip gloss on my lips and dressed in a tiny white bikini that sets off my newly tanned skin, I go back down to the beach. It takes another thirty minutes to get a shot I like—something that would have been easier if I had one of my preferred photographers around. But I've been taking plenty of selfies over the years, and I finally manage to get an image I'm happy with.

Me, looking out over the ocean, the setting sun in the background. It's not really a happy photo, but that's okay. I'm not particularly happy at the moment. After a silent debate with myself, I type out the caption, *Wish you were here*. Then I turn on the location, tagging the resort.

My heart is beating too fast, my breath coming in harsh inhales as if I've been running. This might all be for nothing. There's no way to tell. Maybe Devan really isn't interested and won't even notice what I've done.

Five minutes later, my phone chirps.

I stare at it a long moment, wondering if I've spent so much time thinking about him, I'm not hallucinating his name coming through as a text. Except, no, I'm not, and yes, Devan has actually texted me.

Devan: I told you it's not safe to tag your location.

I don't pause to consider my response.

Me: Oh no. Do you think someone might show up?

Devan: We talked about this.

Come on. Understand what I'm trying to do. Maybe he just needs a little push? It's got to be a good sign that he's obviously got my account tagged or something, right?

Me: And yet, here I am, tagging my location.

Devan: Are you trying to provoke a response?

Me: Maybe.

Me: Is it working?

I hold my breath, waiting as three dots appear, and then disappear, and appear again. I haven't misread things. I *know* that now. We wouldn't be having this conversation if I had. All that said, I need Devan to take a step further. I need him to give me a sign that this is more than just him being over-protective.

A sign that he actually wants *me*.

Devan: You're the one who left without saying a word.

Devan: You have something to say, say it.

Me: I'd rather talk in person.

Devan: Hazel.

Me: You know where I'm at. Come get me.

He doesn't respond. Not in the next few minutes. Not later that night when I'm tossing and turning and failing to fall asleep because every rustle convinces me that I'm missing a phone notification.

By the next morning, the truth settles in. It's really over. He's probably aggravated as hell that I can't take a hint, and now I've thrown myself at him yet again. God, I really can't take a hint, can I?

I pull on an oversized button-down T-shirt dress and wander down to the restaurant. Ordering myself a pitcher of mimosas might be a tad bit self-destructive because I don't think I'll ever drink them again without thinking of *him*, but the heart wants what the heart wants.

Right now, my heart wants to get messy drunk until I forget all about Devan McGuire.

I get seated in a cute little corner booth. Since drinking without some kind of breakfast is crass, I order pancakes. Out of pure spite, I take a picture of the meal and mimosas and post it on social media, tagging the location again.

After this, I'll stop. I swear I will.

Ultimately, Devan *is* right about it not being particularly safe, especially since I'm alone right now, but I hope he sees this picture, thinks about what he described to me, and gets a legendary case of blue balls.

Except posting that picture makes *me* think about it, so now I'm heartbroken *and* horny, and I have no one to blame but myself.

I'm one drink in and picking at my plate when a shadow falls over me. A very large, very angry shadow. I look up slowly, and maybe I've drank more than I realized because I couldn't possibly be seeing what I think I'm seeing.

I blink. "Devan?"

CHAPTER 18

*D*evan looks like he wants to haul me over his shoulder like he did every other time he showed up somewhere unexpectedly, but I'm no longer his ward—not by any stretch of the definition—and it's not my birthday. He plants his hands on the table and leans over it. "Move over."

I'm obeying before I have a chance to decide if I *want* to obey. "What are you doing here?"

"You said you want to talk in person." He scoots into the booth next to me, his big body crowding me in a way that's far too pleasant. "So talk."

"But…" I can't think with him so close, with his thick thigh pressing against mine. "But why?"

"Hazel." Devan eyes my mimosa like it did him personal harm. "I am not a good guy. It took everything I had to let you walk away and not haul you home to chain you up in my office or some shit until you admitted this thing between us was never meant to be temporary. I let you go." He practically growls the last sentence. "Then, two weeks later, you're tagging your location while wearing a little cock-tease of a bikini that I can clearly see your nipples through, and texting me shit about how we should talk in person."

"But—"

"I'm not finished."

I snap my mouth shut. I wanted him to take a step. I should have bargained on Devan doing it in his own way. He looks at me like he wants to memorize every inch of me. "Then I show up here to find you having *brunch* with a whole pitcher of those fancy fruity drinks."

"Mimosas," I whisper.

"Mimosas." He nods. "Wearing a dress that has a man like me wondering what you've got underneath. So talk fast, Hazel. Because it sure as fuck looks like you want the same thing I do."

"What do you want?"

He plants his big hand on my thigh, high enough that his pinkie dips beneath the hem of my dress. "I want everything. I want all your days and your nights. All the fantasies and nightmares. All the goddamned brunches. Everything, Hazel." He doesn't move. "So, if that's not what you're offering, now's a good time to tell me to get the fuck away from you."

This is happening. He's here, saying the things I desperately wanted him to say the day I left things unfinished in the hotel room. I lick my lips and place my hand on Devan's where it sits on my bare thigh. "That's what I want. All of that. Everything."

"Mean what you're saying, birthday girl. Because if I slip my hand up your skirt and find you wet and waiting for me, I'm liable to put a ring on your finger and a baby in your belly the first fucking chance I get."

"Do you promise?"

He makes a sound that sounds almost pained and then he's sliding his hand up my thigh to cup my pussy. I wore panties today, but that only makes it readily apparently how soaked I already am just from thinking about Devan and mimosas earlier.

He doesn't take his gaze from my face as he drags a finger up the center of my panties. "You feel pretty fucking wet, Hazel. I'm still going to need you to tell me yes."

"Is that a proposal?"

"No." He shakes his head sharply. "When I propose, it will be when we're both ready. That doesn't change the fact that saying yes to me means we're headed in that direction. This isn't a fling or a quick fuck. Not for me."

"It isn't for me, either." I bite my bottom lip and fight to keep from spreading my legs. We're tucked back from the rest of the dining room, but that doesn't change the fact that Devan is slowly rubbing his finger up and down my pussy while we're in public. The table mostly hides what he's doing, but if I start riding his hand and moaning, there will be no hiding *that*.

I reach up and cup his face, pausing to relish that I can touch him like this. "I want everything, too, Devan. I want every single fucking day of a happily ever after with you. I want the fights and the making up and the hard days and the easy days. I just want *you*."

He leans down. His lips touch mine as the same moment that he pushes two fingers into my pussy. It's a relatively chaste kiss, completely at odds with the way he's working me between the table. "I love you."

"I love you, too." Words I said on accident before. Ones I'm saying intentionally now.

Devan leans back, stilling his hand as the waitress approaches. She gives us a bright smile, obviously having no idea what my new brunch companion is doing between my thighs. "Welcome. Would you like the menu?"

"Actually—"

"Do you have biscuits and gravy?" Devan cuts me off. When the waitress nods, he gives her a small smile. "I'd like an order of that with coffee, please."

"Coming right up."

I barely wait for her to leave before I glare at him. "I want to go up to the room."

"Yeah, well, *I've* wanted access to this pretty pussy for the last two weeks. A little suffering never hurt anyone."

I drag in a breath that almost—*almost*—comes out as a moan. "I was miserable, too, you know. You weren't suffering alone."

"I know that now." He shifts his hand up a little to rub my clit. "But that doesn't change the fact that I'm going to keep my hand right here until I'm finished eating, and then we're going to go upstairs and I'll have second breakfast."

My laugh comes out a little too high. "You *would* be a *Lord of the Rings* fan."

"Come on, Hazel. You know you are, too." He leans down until his lips brush the shell of my ear. "Just like we both know you're more of a Gimli girl than one who drops her panties for pretty elves."

I can hardly think with him stroking my clit. "You're prettier than Gimli."

"Taller, too." He works three fingers into me. "Now be a good girl and stop squirming. I see my food coming and I don't want to be distracted."

"*You* don't want to be distracted?"

"Exactly."

The next twenty minutes are pure delicious agony. I drink another mimosa as Devan alternates pulsing his fingers inside me and idly stroking my clit. By the time he takes care of the bill, I'm shaking so hard, I'm not sure I can stand. I'm not about to let that stop me, though.

I all but drag Devan to the elevators. He barely waits for

the doors to slide shut and me to press the button for my floor before he picks me up and pins me to the wall, kissing me, deep and harsh. His cock is a hard length between my thighs, a promise of things to come. I don't want to wait. I'm about to say as much when the doors ding open again on my floor.

He doesn't put me down. He simply carries me out and pauses our kiss long enough to say. "Room number." I rattle it off and then he's carrying me down the hall to the room. I fumble the key, and he grabs the card out of my hand, unlocking the door and sending us tumbling inside. He barely pauses to kick it shut behind us when he all but tosses me onto the bed. "Show me."

I yank up my dress and spread my thighs. He never fixed my panties, so they're still bunched on the side, leaving my pussy on display. Devan curses. "Looks like someone is needy."

"You have no idea."

"I think I do." He sinks to his knees at the edge of the mattress and yanks off my panties. I barely have time to brace before he's diving down, kissing my pussy in a borderline frenzy. He's kept me on the edge too long. I want to hold out, but the first time he sucks on my clit, my back bows and I orgasm so hard, my legs shake. "Devan!"

"I missed you."

I give a choked laugh. "Are you talking to me or my pussy?"

"Both." He leverages himself up and undoes the buttons of my dress to my waist, tugging the fabric aside to expose my bare breasts. He shakes his head slowly. "Trust you to wear something deceptively modest and actually be naked beneath it."

"I like easy access." I arch my back. "I missed you, too, you know. A lot."

He pulls his shirt over his head and tosses it behind him. His shorts and underwear quickly follow. Devan hooks me around the waist and drops to the bed, pulling me astride him. "Show me."

I roll my hips, rubbing myself up and down his hard length. I'd half convinced myself that I imagined how big his cock was, but somehow it seems even bigger than I remember. "Did you delete the video of you fucking me in the bathroom?"

"I should have." His gaze drops to my pussy. "If I was a good guy, I would have."

I'm so very fucking glad he didn't. I angle my hips to edge his cock to my entrance. He watches me fight his size to work myself down his length with a satisfied smirk. I love it. I also can't help ribbing him just a little. "How many times did you jack yourself to that video?"

"Enough that both cock and palm got raw." He says it without a hint of embarrassment. "Didn't come close to the real thing."

I swivel my hips, taking him deeper. He's filling me so much, it takes a moment before I'm able to speak again. "I did the same with my video. Rode my hand over and over again, pretending it was yours." One last inch and he's seated entirely within me. Too much, too full, too fucking big, and I wouldn't have it any other way. I brace my hands on his chest and shiver. "Devan?"

"Yeah?"

I start to ride him. "How does your pussy feel?"

His lips curve even as his eyes go hot. "Wet and tight and made just for me."

The desire is there to pick up my pace, to fuck him with all the frenzy of the built-up weeks. I don't. I ride his cock slowly, making the same promise with my body that I made with my words. *Forever.* Not just a day, a weekend, even a month. I'm promising him my future in the same way he's promising me his.

I unbutton my dress and shrug it off. Immediately, his eyes got to my hips, to the faint black marks there. He brushes his thumb over one and his eyes go wide. "Hazel."

"Mmmm?"

"Am I seeing things, or did you *tattoo* my fingerprints on your skin?"

I bite my bottom lip and still my hips. "They were going to fade. I thought I wouldn't ever see you again and I couldn't stand the thought of your marks fading. So I did something about it."

He brushes his thumb over the mark again. "I must be a monster, because I fucking love this so much."

"I love you," I say simply.

He tangles one hand in my hair and tows me down for a kiss. "Say it again," he growls against my lips.

"I love you." Another orgasm is building, a deeper one. I pick up my pace a little, grinding my clit against his stomach. "I love you, I love you, I love you."

Devan rolls me, picking up that same devastating pace that sends me closer and closer to the edge. "I love you, too, Hazel. So fucking much." He grinds down into me and it's too much. I orgasm with his name on my lips. A few harsh thrusts later, he follows me over the edge.

He drops down next to me, tucking me against his side. It takes several long moments before our harsh breathing evens out. Devan presses a kiss to my temple. "I meant what I said. I want to marry you. Eventually do the kids thing if you're not opposed to the idea."

I cuddle closer. Even in my darkest days, I knew I wanted kids eventually. Having them with Devan? I smile against his chest. "I'm not opposed to the idea...eventually."

"No rush. On any of it." There's the faintest hint of hesitation in his tone.

That brings my head up. "You aren't doubting me, are you?"

He smiles slowly. "Never that. But there's no rush on any of it. I love you. You love me. That's enough for me right now."

"Liar." I say it fondly. Having him so close and not kissing him seems a damned shame, so I do. It's slowing dawning on me that I can kiss Devan McGuire whenever I please. The thought makes me dizzy. "I never knew you had a breeder fetish, but you're going to be talking about putting a baby in me every time you get feeling possessive."

He grins against my lips. "Maybe."

"Definitely." I grab one of his hands and guide it between my thighs. "Make me come again, Devan. Twice wasn't anywhere near enough."

"What will be enough for you, birthday girl?" He doesn't immediately start fucking me with his fingers, instead idly stroking my pussy in a way that suggests he's not in any rush. I like it. I like it a lot. Devan kisses my neck. "Five? Ten?"

"I'm kind of afraid I'll never get enough of you." I spread my legs wider. "And it's not my birthday anymore."

Devan rolls me onto my back and moves down my body to settle between my thighs. The grin he gives me is downright wicked. "When you're with me, every day's your birthday, Hazel. Whatever you want is yours."

"That's easy. All I want is you."

* * *

THANK you so much for reading Seducing My Guardian! I hope it brought you a delicious escape from the real world! If you enjoyed it, please consider leaving a review.

· · ·

NEED MORE of Devan and Hazel in your life? If you sign up for my newsletter, you get access to a sexy bonus short from Devan's point of view!

IF YOU'RE LOOKING for more taboo content, be sure to check out Your Dad Will Do! When Lily catches her fiancé cheating, she knows there's only one way to get revenge...seduce her fiancé's father. After this weekend, her ex won't be the only one calling his father Daddy!

* * *

CHECK out this little sneak peek of Your Dad Will Do!

How does one go about seducing their almost-father-in-law? I really, truly do not recommend doing an internet search. The results are heavy on porn and light on answers. In the end, I'm left to my own devices.

That's how I end up on his front porch in a short black dress and thigh highs in the middle of January, well after the polite hours of visiting. I'm shaking as I knock on the door, and it's not purely because the icy wind making my clothing feel like a laughable barrier.

Despite the late hour, he's awake. My breath catches in my throat as the door opens to reveal him. Shane. The man who, up until a few days ago, was supposed to be my father-in-law. Funny how quickly things change when you least expect it. Or not so funny at all. I sure as hell don't feel like laughing.

He fills the doorway, a large man with broad shoulders, big hands, and a smattering of salt and pepper in his hair. He's in his late forties, some twenty-ish years older than me. Shane frowns as recognition slips over his handsome face. "Lily? What are you doing here?"

"I was hoping we could talk." I have to clench my jaw to keep my teeth from chattering. Maybe I should have gone with the trenchcoat route. At least then I'd have a coat.

To his credit, Shane doesn't make me wait. He moves out of the way and holds the door open so I can walk past him. The first blast of warmth makes me shiver again. Maybe if I hadn't stood out there for so long, gathering my courage, I wouldn't be so cold now.

"What did he do?"

I blink and stop trying to rub feeling back into my fingertips. "Excuse me?"

"My asshole son. What's he done now?" He catches my hand and lifts it between us. My ring finger is markedly empty. Shane skates his thumb across the bare skin, still frowning. Now my shivers have very little to do with temperature and everything to do with desire.

Maybe this is why Max and I were never going to work. His freaking father can do more with a single swipe of his thumb than Max was ever interested in doing with his entire body. Then again, Max and I only ever had polite, friendly sex—which was *not* what I found him doing with his secretary when I showed up unexpectedly at his office. I don't want to get into it right now. I've already had four days of tears and raging with my girlfriends, but if I start talking about how I found Max fucking his secretary like the biggest goddamn cliché in existence, I'm going to start crying again.

That's not why I'm here.

I'm here for revenge—and maybe a little pleasure, too, though the pleasure rates a distant second in priorities.

"Shane." I say his name slowly. In all the time I dated Max, I called him Mr. Alby. A necessary distance between us, a reminder of what he was to me—only ever my boyfriend's father. I rip down that distance now and stare up at him, letting him see the pent up emotions I've spent two long years ignoring and denying.

His dark eyes go wide and then hot before he shutters his response, locking himself up tight. But, almost as if he can't resist, he swipes the pad of his thumb over my bare ring finger again. "Tell me what happened."

"We're over." My voice catches, and I hate that it catches. "No going back, no crossing Go, no collecting two hundred dollars. Really, really over."

He nods slowly and then gives my hand a squeeze. "Sounds like you could use a drink."

"I could use about ten, but one's a good place to start." At least he isn't kicking me out. That's a good sign, right? I follow him to the kitchen and watch as he opens the liquor cabinet and picks through the bottles. "Vodka, right?"

"Yes." Of course he's remembers my drink. I bet, if pressed, he also remembers my birthday and a whole host of other details that slip past most people. But then, Shane isn't most people.

Heat melts into my bones as he methodically puts together a drink for each of us. I don't know what to do with my hands once I don't need them for warmth, and the coziness of the temperature is a vivid reminder of just how little I'm wearing. My dress is barely long enough to cover the tops of my thigh-highs and while I'm wearing a garter belt, I have nothing else on beneath the thin fabric of the dress. I'm dressed slutty and downright scandalous and Shane has barely looked at me since I walked through the door.

That won't do. That won't do at all.

He finishes with the drinks and I gather what's left of my courage and close the distance between us, sliding between him and the counter to reach for the glass. "Thank you," I say over my shoulder.

Just like that, he's pressed against my back, his hips

against my ass. He inhales sharply, but doesn't move back. "What are you doing, Lily?"

His lack of retreat gives me a little more strength. Just enough to sip the drink and then turn slowly to face him. I have to lean back over the counter to meet his gaze, and a thrill goes through me as he forces *me* to make the adjustments. He might as well be made from stone. I tip my chin up. "I have a question."

"Ask it."

"Last summer, you and Max were supposed to be working, so I was here at the pool." I can barely catch my breath. "No one was around so I didn't bother with a suit."

"Mmm." The barely banked heat in his gaze is back, flaring hotter by the second. He still hasn't moved, either to press against me or to retreat. "That's not a question."

I lick my lips. "It felt wicked to be out there naked, knowing I was in your house even if you weren't here. I…" This part's harder, but his nearness gives me a boost of bravado. "I started touching myself. I felt like such a little slut, but that made it hotter."

He's breathing harder now, and he reaches around me to grasp the counter on either side of my hips. "Why are you telling me this?"

"Because it's not anything you don't already know," I whisper. "You were upstairs. I saw you watch me through the master window." I reach behind me to the counter just inside his hands. The move arches my back and puts my breasts almost within touching distance of his chest. "I didn't know you were there when I started, but once I knew you were watching me, I took my time and dragged it out. I wanted you to watch. I wanted you to do more than watch." The last I've never admitted to myself, let alone out loud, but it's the truth. "Do you remember that?"

He exhales harshly. "You don't know what you saw."

"Okay." I'm shaking like a leaf. "My mistake."

Shane still doesn't move away. "Even I came home for lunch unexpectedly that day, you were dating my son." He shifts forward the barest amount, closing in on me. "It would be fucked up if I stood in my master bedroom and watched you finger that pretty little pussy. I'd be a monster to have watched the entire thing and fucked my hand while I pretended it was you."

"Shane," I say his name like a secret, just between us. "I'm not dating your son right now."

"What did he do?"

"I don't want to talk about it."

He shakes his head slowly. "You came here with a purpose, but you don't get to throw yourself at me without sharing the truth. Out with it, Lily. What did Max do?"

I really, really don't want to talk about it, but the sheer closeness of him makes my verbal brakes disappear. I find myself answering without having any intention of doing so. "He slept with his secretary. I think he wanted me to catch him. Either that, or he's just really shitty as hiding it when he's up to no good."

He curses softly. "I'm sorry."

"I'm not." It's even the truth. I will cry and I will grieve for the future I thought would be mine, and I sure as hell will spitefully fuck Max's dad, but I'm not sorry I avoided tying my life to someone who never should have been more than a friend.

I lift myself onto the counter, putting us at nearly the same height. The move has my skirt rising dangerously, flashing my thigh-highs and garters.

Shane looks down and goes still. We both hold our breath as he shifts one hand to bracket my thigh and traces the point where my garter connect with the stockings. "Lily." This time, when he says my name, he sounds different.

Almost angry. "If I push up your skirt, and I going to find your bare pussy?"

The words lash me and I can't help shivering. I lick my lips again. "If you want to find out, I won't stop you."

"Dirty girl." He snaps the garter, the sting making me jump. "You came here for revenge."

There's no point in denying it. "Yes."

"I'd have to a selfish asshole to take advantage of you when you're like this." But he's looking at me in the way I've always fantasized about, like he has a thousand things he wants to do to my body and hasn't decided where he wants to start.

"It's what we both want, isn't it?" When he doesn't immediately answer, I press. "Why *not* do it?"

He moves his hand to my hip and grips the fabric of my dress, pulling it tight against my body. "I could think of a few reasons. You were going to marry my son."

I can't quite catch my breath. "I'm not going to now."

"You're young enough to be my daughter."

I watch the dress inch up my legs with every pull of his hand, baring more and more of me. The sight makes me giddy. It's the only excuse for what slips out in response. "Should I call you Daddy, then?"

He goes still. Just like that, he releases my dress and the fabric falls back to cover most of my thighs. Disappointment sours my stomach, but he's not moving back. He skates his hand up my side barely brushing the curve of my breast before he grips my chin just tightly enough to hurt. "Is that what you want, Lily?" He presses two fingers to my bottom lip and I open for him. "You want to call me Daddy while I do filthy things to you that you've only fantasized about." He slips his fingers into my mouth, in and out, in and out, miming fucking. I watch him with wide eyes, but I don't get a chance to decide if I like it or not before he clamps his

141

remaining fingers tightly around my chin, his fingers almost deep enough to gag me.

Shane leans down and holds my gaze as his fingers pulse. "You want to call me Daddy while I slip my hand up your skirt and find out what you have waiting for me? While I bend you over this counter and fuck you with my tongue until you come?" It's almost too much, I can't quite catch my breath, I really *am* going to gag, but he gives me no relief. "You want to ride *Daddy's* cock?"

READ Your Dad Will Do now!

ABOUT THE AUTHOR

Katee Robert is a *New York Times* and USA Today bestselling author of contemporary romance and romantic suspense. *Entertainment Weekly* calls her writing "unspeakably hot." Her books have sold over a million copies. She lives in the Pacific Northwest with her husband, children, a cat who thinks he's a dog, and two Great Danes who think they're lap dogs.

www.kateerobert.com

Keep up to date on all new release and sale info by joining Katee's NEWSLETTER!

Made in the USA
Middletown, DE
05 April 2021